THE LAST HOURS
OF SANDRA LEE

The Last Hours
of Sandra Lee

WILLIAM SANSOM

An Atlantic Monthly Press Book

LITTLE, BROWN AND COMPANY
BOSTON   **TORONTO**

LIBRARY OF CONGRESS CATALOG CARD NO. 62-8066

FIRST AMERICAN EDITION

ATLANTIC—LITTLE, BROWN BOOKS
ARE PUBLISHED BY
LITTLE, BROWN AND COMPANY
IN ASSOCIATION WITH
THE ATLANTIC MONTHLY PRESS

*Published simultaneously in Canada
by Little, Brown & Company (Canada) Limited*

PRINTED IN THE UNITED STATES OF AMERICA

THE LAST HOURS
OF SANDRA LEE

I

Dear Sir,

    With reference to her legs encased in sheerest nylon, she turned the left one over, knees together, parting the flow of shimmering buti-silk boudoir coat in three colours, angel-blue, love-grey and mutation, to expose a cream smooth thigh to Gerald's pulsating gaze. His breath came in sobs as with arms wide Sandra yet averted her lowered eyes, tempting him, so near Gerald so far, while the head-long scent of Shadowsweet No. 2 rose all around to madden his brain, and the long-player throbbed muted strains of *Yours, Yours,*
Yours faithfully,
Sandra (Marjorie) Lee

Her hands dropped from the typewriter keys and her eyelids, loaded with green grease, raised themselves to let water-wet eyes look through the window at white tiles all over the office well.

Beyond, where endlessly the range of grimed dairy-like bricks ended, a grey December sky flooded down cold light: inside, behind her, the grey suits of men were bowed over grey letters, ledgers.

It was the end of another year.

'Grey skies grey as my eyes,' Sandra suddenly sang at the blank sheet of writing-paper, 'snap out of it.'

Because, however long the year had been, it was going to be a long day today. It was Friday, December the

Twenty-third. It was the day of the Office Party. The afternoon would be a rout, a riot. Already it was absurd to call the office grey, for round each desk and in drawers everywhere there lay parcels and tissue-wrapped bottles, and where these touched a radiator the heat sent out festive crackle-sounds of crinkly paper, red and green Christmas crackle.

Yet—would she, she Sandra, ever see this Party?

Her heart gulped again, right into her throat, as it had all morning, to think of what was most momentous! Her boy, her man, her Bun asking her to throw up everything, to leave at lunch, to drive away with him and get married to him! That very day! Or at least to face together her parents today and then start seeing registrars and things about a quick wedding soon after Christmas. Bun had to go and lay electric cables all over Sarawak. That was why.

And she was not sure. It had all boiled up and over too quick. How could a girl say Yes so suddenly? Especially to a man she knew so well over so many years. Especially, yes, to a steady—so steady they had never even bothered to get engaged.

Quiet bell-sounds punctured the rubbery office air as typing and duplicating machines chattered to and fro: and underneath and away, like the pounding of engine-room pistons, a muffled thumping of deep motor traffic blotted up any edges of silence. A light smell arose from paper, ribbon-ink, pencils, lubricating oil and from the extra-ordinary metal presence, like the slow thick taste of tin on the tongue, of the filing cabinets.

Moreover, she was already dated to lunch with Nevile

Wrasse, with dark-eyed Nevile who would drive her in his low white car to a smart lunch in the powder-scented West End.

There indeed was a problem. And it was marked now or never, neck and crop, neck or nothing. Not that Nevile mattered. It was the Decision that mattered. And Bun would be ringing at eleven. If then she said Yes, she must leave at lunch and not come back, Goodbye to all and Hello Sarawak.

Yet how to take the final step?

There was, at least, half an hour yet. Better to think? Better not to think?

She looked down at the paper beneath her on which was typed, under a stamped letter-heading THE ALLASOL MISSION LTD., simply: 'Dear Sir, With reference to' and the rest of the page mind-blank.

But then as she raised her hands to begin once again, she saw a purple ribbon-stain on her oyster-grey index nail. Automatically the other hand reached down and took from the drawer a little bottle of nicotine-remover, fluffed some into cotton-wool—and then dropped a drop of remover down on to her lap. The wet drop stared up from among the many polka-dots that made up the pattern of her dress.

'Oh no,' she said.

And added, 'Oh no, Sandra!' as she foresaw the big pale rim with which this fierce stain-remover would stain her dress and began to worry: Will another spot matter among all these real spots, will it ever be seen? It had fallen on a nasty awkward place, though. She needed a mirror and rose to leave for what at Allasol they called the Red Hell—the Staff Powder Room.

She rose from her small square nest of dark wood desk, wire baskets, piled paper, and the big grey typewriter, to stand fleshy and exotic against a wall of mud-green steel files. Her hair, dyed bright brown and piled into a strange sharp fashionable shape, her silk-seeming dress and stockings, her high shoes and low neck played a most female essence against the dry office furnitures. In the cold light shed from white tiles outside, make-up made a mask of her face, for each layer of unguent or powder intended for tender café-light became as individually marked as the painted stripes on the face of a celebrant savage. It was difficult in any light ever to know what her face was doing beneath this mask, it was so thick and static that only tears or smiling teeth could send forth recognisable signals.

She passed between old Miss Cook in her fussy, cardiganed corner and the desks of Mr Mansford and big Mr Tiny Hearst, who stood together conferring over some photographic enlargements spread out on Mansford's desk.

But perceiving an atmosphere of gossip rather than work, she paused.

'It's nothing to do with us, is it old man?' said Mansford, a good-looking young man, darkly brilliant like a pirate, but who was contentedly married and thus looked wrong and wasted.

Big pink-and-white-faced Tiny Hearst lowered his pale porker's eyes and echoed Mansford's words, drawing back his head a few inches the better to survey the photographs:

'We're old enough to know better, aren't we old man?'

'In her birthday suit, eh?'

'In the buff.'

'And to think that the original of this, ahem, Art Study is now sitting large as life, one floor beneath us in the typing pool!'

'They have to strip to type down there? Didn't know the old pool was wet as that.'

Sandra (Marjorie) Lee leaned forward by Ralph Mansford to peep-bo at the photographs. They showed the back of a naked young woman, squatting so that her bottom should not show too much, and the outline of one breast showing round from the front, but with the nipple painted off.

'You mean that's Sue Blair, is it really?' she asked, eyelids working up and down. 'However could she? In the office, too.'

'In the Studio,' Mansford said. 'She went along with the P.R.M. to take notes and the model didn't turn up so Sue volunteered.'

'No!'

'Yes.'

Hearst put in: 'Took off her thingummies there and then and click, it was all over. Painless and professional. They say she's done it before.'

'Sue Blair's been done like that before?' said Sandra, a kind of hot envy rising through her first shock.

'Magazines, they say. Thumbies.'

9

'What?'

'What you thumb over when the bookseller isn't looking.'

Sandra put a look of shock across her face, and raised her voice:

'Well, of all the barefaced—'

The two men turned and looked at her hard.

From elderly Miss Mavis Cook's corner, from her 'little home' made up of a calendar of bluebells and a cardigan on a hanger and a big red tartan biscuit-tin, a lightly laughing voice pealed to the rescue:

'Really, if the girl wants to make an exhibition of herself, then let her, say I. And after all, if she's got a lovely body . . . we've all got bodies, haven't we?'

There was silence.

'We-ell,' said Sandra, 'she looks kind of cold for Christmas. My, I must run!' and she had already taken six quick tight-skirted steps onwards to the Powder Room when there came a shout from a door among glass partitions behind.

'Marge!' a smart auburn-haired woman cooed at her. 'Here a second, can you?'

'Damn her,' thought Sandra, who had changed her name from Marjorie only a year before, and to whom the word Marge now cut like fingernails on glass. But she instantly smiled, 'Coming!' and tacked quickly over towards this Monica Naseby, who was H. J.'s personal assistant, and who had emphasised the forbidden name on purpose. Monica was thirty, and thus ripe enough to scorn all affectation in the young.

'Hell and hell and hell,' Sandra-Marge thought, as she looked down quick again at the stain-remover spot, which was already drying—but all her teeth opened in sweetness:

'Sure, Monny, what can I do you for?'

She passed within the glass partition which served as a protective vestibule to the closed polished doors of the directors' rooms beyond.

'Mr Deane,' said Miss Naseby, pinning papers together offhand, 'said you had asked to leave early, before lunch. He says Yes, all right, only wanted a word with you first.'

'Oh—now?'

Monica now came smiling through official Miss Naseby. Very regular pearly teeth arrived among dimples strongly assuring benevolence, as, upon embracing you, a python might smile.

'Really, Marge, you shouldn't worry Mr Deane with staff details. He's got more than enough, especially as we're hurrying to clear the decks for the Party. Come to me next time, eh?'

Nothing showed through Sandra's mask but again smiling teeth—and what finally is a smile but a kind of bite, loving or not?

'Don't I know,' she agreed, 'but I was just with him, and I thought not to appear rude missing his Personal Message—'

'Of course, love,' said Monica to cut her short, and rose like a chic tube in her dark career suit to go and tap on H. J.'s door. Here and there the tube was slightly swollen, as if a woman inside was waiting to flower after hours.

Sandra looked down at her spot, and the thoughts pounded into an agonising race. What was he asking her in for? Was it to receive her Personal Message now, as it were, personally? For the Personal Message was the way H. J. liked to think of the Christmas Bonus Packet, which he always delivered in person. And would H. J. see her spot? No, at least not *that*—and she whisked up a sheet of blotting-paper to hold it in place when the call came.

And what—worst of all, was she going to say about going off early? Because she had asked about this only because of Bun and his idea to drive straight off—and she had asked it particularly casually, as a possibility, as a perhaps. After all—she had not made up her mind herself. But now was H. J. about to expand it into a concession? Was it to be Yes or No in the next two or three minutes? It seemed like Fate forcing her hand. But did she like Fate forcing her? No, unless she had already made up her own mind, when Fate became a different matter, less a force than a helping hand itself.

Because if she went to lunch with Bun she would not only be missing the Party if not also the Personal Message, but missing as well what was much more important and fluttered and banged against her mind this morning like a cloud of big moths—missing Life.

It had been terribly plain from Bun's new stern look and from a kind of extension to his jaw, as if he were throttling on a collar-stud, that it was for Life this time. Marriage, it was. And that would be wonderful, it was where deeply and happily with Bun she wished to head.

And Sarawak, perhaps, was wonderful too. But it would be all twice as wonderful if something had *happened* first. Or if there were time yet for something to happen. Something. Anything. An event, a romance, an accident, a 'something' to look back upon. Something outrageous, something terrible, something exciting, something even just bad.

For life had been pretty uneventful. Despite her appearance, which differed little from how a whore might be thought to look, Sandra was a good girl. And she was already twenty-two years old. While one side of her sent a white Sandra willingly pure into her future husband's arms, another side deplored this. Should so much be sacrificed all at once? All the desires and dreams of her growing years, all she had tended so carefully in mirrors everywhere, all the Sandra she had made, inside and out? Marriage, they say, is an adventure. But it did not seem to have quite the line of other adventures. Desperately she wished for some kind of a past with which to face the future.

Then H. J.'s door began to open—just as a big girl came whisking past in a glow of pink-washed cheeks and rose-fresh powder. Fine strong calves halted, sensibly-pleated skirt swirled to a stop as Jill Jenkins, her desk-neighbour, paused to whisper at Sandra's ear:

'Has your Bun phoned yet?'

Sandra shook her head, and pointed a finger at the door. Jill smiled her huge fresh smile, tossed back chestnut curls and whispered:

'Who's a now-or-never girl? Why, Sandra Sarawak!'

And bounced off humming the first bars of the Wedding March.

'Now or never' drummed at her mind as she went forward to H. J.'s room, and whether it was the predicament itself or the predicament plus the spot on her dress, or other things as well, like the sudden strong daylight striking in from H. J.'s door and blinding her, and a ruck in the carpet that gave a tug at her heel that tugged right up to her suspender-belt—she suddenly flushed with quick anger: 'Why, it's wrong a man should lay down terms like that. Shouldn't he be on his knees asking? Who is this Bun? Where is this Sarawak?'

'Yes, Mr Deane?'

'Miss Lee? Yes.'

They were alone. Godfrey Deane, a big-built man whose initials H. J. stood for Honest Jack, a device of the staff born of the large twinkle he put into eyes to simulate cleanliness and frankness in the murky business of merchandising—this big good-looking fifty-year-old leaned athletically back in his chair, arms wide on the chair-arms, all chest and tie, and twinkled.

'Can you keep a secret, Miss Lee?'

Holding her blotter casually in place, Sandra thought quickly what to say. Say, cynically, 'I'm a woman, Mr Deane.' Say, jollily, 'Cross my heart, Mr Deane.' Say, poker-faced, 'What's it worth to you, mister?'

'A *secret*, Mr Deane?' she said.

A tired look of wear and tear washed the twinkle from Mr Deane's eye.

'I see I can trust you. It's just this,' he said, and upended a small envelope with a significant finger, then let it drop as though worthless. 'It's the bonus. We've not had a bad year, but, quite frankly, it's not come up to expectations. We've all got to tighten our belts that much. I'm afraid this—which we offer you now with our best wishes for a Happy Christmas—is only half what you might usually expect.'

Sandra's make-up stood her in good stead. Not a sign of disappointment showed through. And she managed to say, evenly:

'I'm only sorry for Allasol's sake, Mr Deane,' while Half-oh-God-Half wailed at the back of her quite honest concern for the Company.

But now Mr Deane was writing on the packet, and at the same time extending his free hand towards her stomach.

'Blotter,' he said. 'I've lost my ballpoint.'

Panicked, she drew it back. Then fearfully extended the blotting-paper. It was awful. And the cold grey sunlight blinding her through the window.

'I've added—and a Happy New Year. I hope it will be, for all of us. I've great plans for expansion. You know, Miss Lee, when we first formed Allasol, it was to be called Allasol Beauty Products Ltd. But that did not seem enough. It had to be bigger—and finer. You know, The Allasol Group of Companies, the Allasol Organisation, Allasol Initiatives. Something that had—well, call it class. Call it dignity.'

He leaned even further back, staring vaguely at her

stomach. A visionary blur clouded his eyes:

'And then I thought, the thought came to me, Miss Lee —The Allasol Mission! And so it was. And that's just what we are—a mission, we have a mission to perform for our public. And so if we all pull our weight—but I need say no more to *you*, Miss Lee, need I?'

And back came the twinkle while his eye searched her up and down for one of the personal and friendly touches with which he believed the staff were welded to the firm's inmost fibre.

'That's a pretty dress you have on,' he said, and clamped his twinkle right on the spot itself, where now her hands were clasped. 'And that's oyster Sleek if I'm not mistaken. Good match.'

He had only seen Allasol's polished grey varnish on her nails! God bless Allasol. But he was continuing:

'When I said a "secret", I meant just don't tell anyone about the bonus for a moment. It's better coming from me, when I come round this afternoon. I don't want to put too much of a damper on the Party. Advance information to you only because you're leaving early.'

And suddenly, looking at him there, the hard-wearing big man with his bony brow and strong black eyebrows, she noticed in that cold daylight that his hair was thinning in front, and she thought: The cares and worries of the poor man. And she said:

'No, Mr Deane, I want to stay. I'm very sorry Allasol's in such straits. I'm staying right here to help make the Party go.'

A flush of loyalty coloured down on her neck below

the white mask, which stayed white, so that for a moment she looked terribly pale, about to faint. But that was not the reason for a startled light in H. J.'s eye.

'Now don't be saying we're in straits, Miss Lee! This is a purely domestic matter. Within these four walls—you understand? It's just that for once we can't pass so much on. We're consolidating. And expanding.'

'I quite understand, Mr Deane,' she said firmly, and felt a grave welling of tears, as at an anthem.

'See you later, then,' he said, and nodded as he picked up the photographs of Sue Blair's back. 'I've got to get these Shadowsweet displays decided before we . . . hm . . .'

Deftly she turned and left, her chin high with pride. But once through the glass vestibule and into the paler world of the outer office her new loyalty remembered the old.

'Oh, what have I done? That's done Bun. I can't go early now,' and her heart gave its great gulp again.

'Hi, Sandra, quick—it's your Bun,' Jill called from the telephone between their desks. 'I've been holding the fort—what've you two been doing in there, founding a family? No, not you Bun,' she said to the receiver. 'Private call too, quick!'

Dazed, with bridges burned, Sandra took up the telephone firmly and angrily:

'Sandra here. Bad news, Bun, I can't get away. No . . . it's too difficult. . . . Let nothing what stand in the way? Not at a moment like this? Well, Bun, there are moments and moments is all I can say. Mm . . . I know dear, and

I'm terribly terribly sorry. Really I am. Well if *that's* all you can say, you can ring right off. . . . No, I've *not* got the curse!'

She banged down the receiver—muttering 'Curse, *curse* it,' to cover that word and sucking her finger as if she had hurt it.

The voice of Miss Cook came evenly across:

'Did Mr Deane actually *ask* you to stay then, dear?' Behind her glasses her eyes looked more than usually anxious.

'Not really, I volunteered because of the bo—' and then her lips snapped holding the secret back. To have forgotten in that short time! But here was another loyalty at stake—here she was against her fellow-workers, with the boss's secret. . . .

'Because of the Party,' she almost shouted. 'Because I'd like to be here, with you all, after the year!'

And she hurried away at last to the Powder Room, though this was no longer necessary, for round a few of the starry spots on her stomach a big white ring now shone, like the ring of a strange new planet.

Jill Jenkins whirled along after her.

'Thank God at last,' Mansford swore, reaching for the free telephone.

He gave the number of a nearby hospital and asked whether there was any news yet? For Mrs Mansford was at that time in labour, and all the morning he had spent dully sharing his wife's agony along with the November figures of a sales survey, angrily wishing to protect her from so cruel an attack from within, tenderly feeling for the sudden defencelessness of women who thus on the brink of motherhood seemed more than ever to be just young girls, and at the same time fearfully suppressing other thoughts that doomily loomed: Will I bear it? The nappies, the prams, the rubber ducks? The school fees? What kind of a dark happiness is this?

'Napoo,' he said brightly to Hearst as he rang off, 'Mafeking not yet relieved.'

Hearst popped out his eyes from under their pale lashes. He smiled a knowing, kindly, curly smile:

'Then perhaps we'd better have a—'

His hand reached down to where a bottle lay ready for the Party. But stopped. It came back to him about last year's party when old Merrydew had thrown the L—M file out of the window, said the President was passing and rated a paper welcome. Lord, what a shambles—and they were jiving like bloody Bacchantes all over the Typing Pool and Mansford had thrown up in Mavis Cook's waste-paper basket, got it all in though, neat job.

No, better not start as early as this.

'I feel wretched,' Mansford muttered.

'The gentlemen,' Mavis Cook said, 'always have the worst of it. I don't suppose anyone has a rubber?'

In the terribly scarlet Powder Room, painted thus by a Time-and-Motion man to keep the staff from spending too much time there, Sandra was dabbing her new ring with water.

19

'It's done for,' she said. 'Water's no good. So do I get another remover to remove the remover? Hell, what a morning.'

'You certainly gave Bun a flea in his ear!' Jill said, looking in the glass at her face dark pink from the red walls. 'I look as if I'd sold my soul to the Devil.'

'I think I have,' Sandra murmured. 'I'm afraid I was all confused about something and then I had to take it out on poor Bun. Still, he needn't have been quite so sure of himself saying a thing like *that*.'

'I could have cried laughing,' Jill giggled.

'Died, dear, died.'

'But Sandra you can understand him. After all—with the car ready and all your plans made.'

'It was always Bun's point,' Sandra said rubbing away, 'that we were to present the parents with the whole idea early today, to drive down now for lunch, give them time. And then go ahead about the licence later in the afternoon.'

'Well he's right, right as a privet, if you're going to get hitched before he flies off.'

'Trivet, Jill. You get your words right, girl—what Bun's *not* right about is giving the parents time. They'll agree like flashes. Good heavens, they're mad about giving their dear daughter her freedom. I think they go away for week-ends specially to leave me the house free to turn into a one-girl brothel—so modern. Trouble is I never have.'

'Sandra!'

'No, I don't mean that. I mean I'm simply not free

enough somehow inside myself, in *here*, Jill. Oh, why do we know so much about ourselves nowadays?'

'I don't know, we know what we're doing, don't we?'

Sandra stood up and went to the glass too, so that two faces stared at each other with the red wall reflected behind.

'I'm not sure I *do* know what I'm doing. I mean, how can I want to marry Bun and then keep putting him off? O Lord, if only something would *happen*!'

Jill said: 'If he wants you, dear, he'll stick. You're in your rights to give him a chase. It's—what is it?—biologically correct.'

'Come again?'

'It's usual. Though there's something unusual about you, my girl. Personally, I hae ma doots.'

'About what?'

'Whether you're really in love with him.'

Sandra gave a weary Oh-sound.

'How *can* you be so obtuse,' she said.

'Eh?'

It was a word she had found in a magazine article. The word had startled her, and stuck. But she was not going to explain it now.

'Anyway,' she said, 'you're not taking the risk—oh my God, look at the time, and I've got seven odourless old Fresh! stickers to finish up before we break.'

'You could come out of this place with red rims round your eyes—I've only got my Sleek to do. But will you go down with Bun later then?'

'I don't know.'

She took a last jabbing dab at her dress. 'I really just don't know.'

Jill-in-the-mirror then put her face forward to look at Sandra closer in that glass.

'Oh, my pet,' she said, 'oh Sandra darling, you're crying. And I thought it was the red.'

'I'm not, I'm not,' Sandra sobbed, 'I'm not,' pursing her lips into a little pudding, and dabbing, dabbing at her spot. 'But I do know *one* thing,' she said, coming to herself, 'I do know I can't go about like *this* all day. For two pins I'd go right out and get another dress. But for the two pins.'

And then she turned to her friend and her lips slowly opened in a big, sly smile:

'Jill,' she said. 'Times are hard. Can you keep a secret?'

II

THERE was yet over an hour until the quarter-to-one lunchers would rise.

For the time being, finishing up work before the whole office more or less broke up for Christmas and their afternoon party, even the women were subdued. Though it would take more than this to subdue their appearance, for the dark files and the bare grey walls provided them with a better background for their bright clothes than ever again in their lives they would have. In no drawing-room, no theatre would they flower as finely as against these masculine neutralities: out of their own, they came into it.

Those three now present, Jill and Sandra and Mavis, sat three in a row against the windows, through which could be seen only those lifeless white-bricked walls, endless other windows, and chimneys remote above. In such cold light, their dresses shone bright as paper flowers.

The two men in sober grey suits sat at rather larger desks under frosted windows each set in a partitioned area. Only there were not yet any partitions built. At the moment a very small, thin man scuttled about their feet on the floor, measuring for carpet and the hardboard which would rise one day to wall in the two managers. This workman wore pads on his knees, and with his thin arms and legs looked like a large spider—he was always on the floor somewhere in Allasol, altering and measuring. It was rumoured that the incessant re-deployment of carpet

23

and partition was also an idea of the Time-and-Motion man, to keep everybody on the move and discourage any too somnolent settling-in.

But to Mansford's right, and opposite the three women, rose permanent and glossy glass partitions enclosing Miss Monica Naseby and the Directors' Doors.

It was now one of those curious periods in which the whole room seemed bent on work, in relative silence. Nor did anyone pass through from the passage outside. The electric clock, with its red second-hand circling silently and remorselessly, became the liveliest thing in the place. Each person there seemed shrunk with inward thinking, isolated: such chance remarks as were from time to time made sounded isolated too, addressed to no one in par-ticular, for the speaker would hardly raise eyes from work.

But the air of concentration was false. Just as that mouse music of small crinkling sounds rose from presents and tissue-wrapped bottles lying near the warm radiators, so lighter thoughts kept rising.

While Mavis Cook typed one of her vintage letters to a recipient of their new fast-staying scent, Longeur—'a remittance for this account would be esteemed a favour'—her mind kept tapping: 'The egg-cups or the straw bread-holder, the egg-cups or the straw? Which would Meg like best? Dare I get a cigar for H. J., for Mr Deane?'

Sandra faced a further sheet, blank but for its lonely Dear Sir, and worried about Bun. Then she began to type hard to suppress a rising panic which might get her into a state.

Mansford was still finalising the November survey of

representative towns in the Midlands and East Anglia, his blood wrestling hot on the bed with his wife's agony.

Hearst was checking estimates for a new plant extension at the Allasol factory, but said aloud:

'I saw a funny thing yesterday.'

Without turning from his papers, Mansford said:

'Why this Lincolnshire strength in all lines? Lipstick, scent, pancake—couldn't it be the Yank air-bases?'

'I saw Father Christmas,' said Hearst.

'You did?' Mansford said, frowning his strong black eyebrows at the survey.

He flexed his lips, showing teeth so white they looked false against his sallow skin. He was a spare gristly man, with strong tendons outlining his neck, and a long brilliantined skull of shoe-black hair: yet straggling dark hair at his wrists gave him a sickly rather than virile look. His sober grey suit drooped with touches of cheap linen—a handkerchief tucked into limp long shirt cuffs, another in his breast-pocket, and a very soft collar.

Hearst sighed and said:

'I saw him. In his red hood and white beard over by Marble Arch. And what happens but round the corner comes a tramp, a real old codger—with a long brown beard and a kind of khaki cape round his head!

'The two of them stop dead at the sight of each other. You never saw anything like it. One coloured, one khaki. Like a soldier back from the front meeting a buddy in scarlet. You could see they smelled trouble—like a couple of dogs. Couple of bad dreams come true. Must have got the shock of their lives.'

'Yes? What happened?'

'Happened?' Hearst pouted, petulant as a big pink baby with his pig-eyes and his pale cropped hair, 'Happened? Isn't that enough?'

'Oh, sure.'

'It was the suspense, I tell you—those two Santas scared out of their wits.'

'I thought you said one wasn't a Santa.'

Hearst gave a weary growl.

Sandra had been half-listening. She agreed with Mansford. She often could not see the point when men talked. It was a relief to find one of them not seeing it too. How did Tiny Hearst get all those scars at the back of his neck? Old boils? My, but he was a big man, she thought with pride. He might have been her father; but she still thought it with pride. Funny, she thought. Men, she thought.

Hearst had cropped hair which looked like a crew cut but was a legacy of much earlier times. He was like an elephant in his grey suit bagging all over. Yet his fingers were small and thin and white, like hairless little parsnips.

'My dear fellow,' he now said in pompous tones retained from his upper schooldays, 'are we quite compos mentis? The cares of fatherhood? Santa's going to pay regard to you this year, my billy-boy.'

The spider on the floor suddenly put in:

'I 'ad twelve.'

Mansford started, and looked down at his trouser cuff, where the sound had come from.

'Eh? Twelve what?'

'Little 'uns. Three passed on. Leaves nine.'

26

'Oh,' said Mansford.

'You may well say that, sir,' said the man, 'that you may well say.'

Mansford coughed and scuffled his papers to imply concentration. The spider went on measuring, the clock circling, the typewriters belling and chuttering. No one spoke for some time. Like the lounge of a residential hotel after voices have momentarily broken the hush, the office expired back into work.

Poor chap, thought Hearst, poor chap. It seems wrong for it to be happening here in the office. You wanted a more conventional figure, tousled male in dressing-gown, whisky bottle. Else how could a fellow tell a chap was having a child? He looked so fit and well.

Meanwhile, he thought, there's this damn party— wonder who's going to blow his top this year? So much to drink—wish I could take a drop too, but needs mustn't when the belly drives. Buy a half of mixed fondants to suck, stick around or you'll never see anything in life. Besides, my pregnant colleague needs an ally at this time.

He picked up a pencil, carefully sniffed the bitter-sweet cedarwood scent—funny how sexy it smells—and put a tick to a covered extension for forty double-stacked bicycles.

Mavis Cook boomed down the telephone:

'Are you there? Yes. We're connected. . . . Mavis here—can you hear me?'

Although she was not yet fifty, Miss Cook had never learned to take the telephone lightly. She still shouted down it as if addressing her caller directly over the miles; and there was an echo of lifeboats and gallant storm-tossed cable-layers in her emergent stress of great distances and perilous connections.

Her voice reached through the glass panels, and Monica Naseby's head turned sharply. She stared at Mavis through the glass, the lift of her chin accusing: 'Another private call!' But she dared not say this directly. Her face framed in the partitioning showed particularly clearly—floury with powder, whitish eye-shadow, thin definite dark lipstick and thinned dark-pencilled eyebrows, under the darkly red hair. A smart woman, one would have said. No nonsense about her. Pearl ear-studs.

'It's the most popular dog-book of the year,' Mavis boomed, 'she'll love it.'

Monica could bear it no longer, she took up a folder from her desk and crashed through the door. She strode over to Mavis's desk and put the folder down.

'Will you *just* see that goes down?' she said.

She paused long enough to show she was not smiling, then swung round and off to avoid any exact riposte from Miss Cook, who was one to stand on her rights if in the wrong.

Used as they were to Miss Naseby, Sandra and Jill watched her depart.

'Silly little legs,' Sandra thought. For Monica had very low knees, which gave her a Central European waddle. Even when hemlines were short, her skirt looked long.

Jill Jenkins sniffed, and then bent closer to see how a second f had got left out of the word 'midriff'. Could this really matter, it looked nicer anyway? While she thought: Christmas! Green holly over the house, bright berries winking, kisstletoe and turkey! And a blazing fire, and the church bells in the morning, Dad and Mummy and the Rogers, Dick and Pam, all in our best, clean and laughing and the lovely nutty taste of sherry and tissue crinkling open by the tinsel-tree! Can it really be only two days off, no, one and a half? Christmas Eve, the breathless dark quiet of it, putting out the pillow-cases for the children, tip-toe quiet in the dark . . . would one ever get to sleep? And how could people grumble about their shopping-feet and all the bother, the way they do, with such wonders about to burst on the smiling firelit morning? Would there be snow? Hurrah!

Thank God there won't be any messy snow this year, Sandra said to a blank white sheet of Allasol paper. 'Dear Sir,' she tapped, and stopped again. She looked over at Jill. Nothing bothers *her*. Not so much as an Oh when I said about the bonus, you can't see anything getting *her* down but she'd come smiling through. She's the real English Rose. Oh, how can I face what's coming to-morrow at my dear home, Bun or no Bun? Another year gone!

Because every year at Sandra's home the three of them, her youthful father and mother and herself, gathered round the glazed mauve tiles of the family hearth and held an investigation into the preceeding twelve months. It was a family institution, half-serious, half-game. Pops would drag at his pipe and look lean and thoughtful,

Mother would sit upright, bright and earnest—and the three would go right over the last year. As usual, Sandra knew she would sit there smiling brightly but thinking really: Nothing nothing *nothing* has happened to *me*.

What had Pops said last time? 'Credit Balance—past forty and I've still got my own teeth. Can still go up the stairs two at a time. Debit—instead of receiving Christmas presents from uncles and aunts, I find myself giving them to nephews and nieces. Young men have started calling me Sir. With a heart still seventeen, I find I've crossed the border into age.'

And Mother? 'O dear now, I might say our holiday at Montreux was the high spot. Or that lovely week-end in Wales. But I'm going to be *honest*—' and she looked round as if all should be astonished at this—'my big moment was when Mrs Jameson left and dear Mrs Cadwaller came to clean the house. That woman's a treasure, Montreux or no Montreux.'

And I, their little Marjorie, what had I to offer but lies? Simpering about my frightful ten days in Brittany where no young man worth a third look offered himself. Making do with a boring Pierre in love with his scooter. Two days in Paris, sitting about hoping for the dark flasher in the white car to appear. And running away terrified at the first sight of one. Ending up sitting in a cinema *alone*! In Paris!

And the feeling of emptiness after what might seem otherwise a full year . . . the slight chain of interested young men, the bubbling beginnings and flat dull skirmishes as one after the other they tried to go too far, and, rejected, lost interest. Bun did not figure among these: he had his separate compartment as an old family friend of years' standing, who had quite quietly flowered in the last two years as her destined suitor.

If, like Mother, she sought for the truth, then the real successes of the year were made up of an enormous white fleecy spring coat, and the new pale grey finely-needled high fidelity record player. This she had sat with for hours, luxuriating in its message of 'contemporary' rightness as much as in the music itself. Add, that beautiful new silvery electric iron of Mother's: just to see it at anchor like a little liner on the ironing board was a pleasure. But how could she talk of such material matters as high points of the year? Whereas people prattled all day for twelve months about their material acquisitions, it was now indecent to mention them.

And suppose she mentioned her two 'fiascos'—which she had not mentioned to a single soul on earth? These she shuddered to think of even to herself, these two low-point episodes of the year. The time she got drunk, and the man with the wig! They were like bad dreams treasured because they were the only dreams you have had.

Staring down at the Allasol letter-head, she put these two to the back of her mind; where their heads bobbed about and lovingly leered. As always, they occasioned the idle, deep thought: 'Who am I, really?'

She looked up alarmed. And what am I doing here, she thought, with Bun in the balance and the clock going round, why don't I make up my mind and just go? Whatever I said to H. J.? Who's H. J.? Who are all these people?

She looked round the office and thought: I know big Tiny Hearst's a widower and lives in West Kensington and eats sweets all day—but little more than that. And Mavis is getting on and lives in a room in Belsize Park and we all sort of hope she and Tiny might one day hit it off— and Mavis has told me all sorts of things, about her knitting and her holiday and her relations, but what does it add up to? I haven't seen with my eyes what their lives are up to. They're a lot of ghosts. Monica Naseby lives at Brighton. But so do thousands of others. What have they got on their mantelpieces in their homes?

She looked round amazed at this last thought. You felt you knew them so well in one way—yet there were all their mantelpieces, which they saw night and morning, which lived with them, and you knew nothing, nothing whatsoever about them!

She looked hard at Ralph Mansford and began to dream—his wife in their three-room flat-in-a-block, all painted cream, room kept empty for the baby, and the sitting-room mantelpiece with, what? Silver cups Ralph had won, a little glassy clock showing its works, the two wedding-present vases shaped like tree-trunks—but of course that was a mantelpiece you remembered from somewhere, not Ralph's at all.

'I don't know,' she sighed aloud, as if at life or the morning, 'I really don't know.'

Jill leaned over to her and sighed:

'Nor do I, dear. You know what you told me about the

you-know-what—I've got to run out at lunch to buy all my last presents, and lord knows what with.'

Sandra looked at her with distaste, almost venom. Lovely hair, if you like chestnut hair that is—but look at those big red ears. The price of an English Rose complexion. And big purple circles under the eyes, puppy-purple. Oh, a girl with a golden heart all right, but a bit too hearty come to that—not like Daphne, dear Daph, who had her head screwed on tight, oh Daph why did you have to go and get married and leave me all alone?

Jill said sternly:

'I shall have to put my thinking cap on, that's all,' as if this garment were not much to her liking.

Daph wouldn't have said that. Daph wore hers day and night—and what were Daph's nights like now? She'd been gone a year last November, thirteen unlucky months, it was like a friend dying the use she was to you any more, and she and Daph were like sisters. Now there was no one to talk to. No one took Daph's place. Yet what had Jill said, come to think of it, something very searching—yes, Jill had her moments, she's rather a dear after all—about Daph?

'You know since your great Daph went off to be married, you've bloomed. Deadly nightshade if you like, but a real lovely new flower you've made of yourself. It's an ill wind, Jill had said, and she was right, for something about Daph going had set her off, she had changed her hairstyle and put an inch on her heels and bought all kinds of new clothes when she could, not nice-style at all but snazzy as tell-your-Mum, in fact she'd even changed her name. It was as if she was the one had gone to get married, not Daph.

Then why had she not gone and married Bun then? Because Bun had no mon. Bun was steady, studying to reap richer rewards in time. Or had she been too young? But twenty-one was an age these days. And people managed on no mon, if they really wanted. Why not then?

I am a coward, she thought. I don't face up to things, I want things then I run away. I'm not a coward for not marrying Bun, because that will certainly come, but I'm a coward for not doing what I'm not marrying Bun for.

What had Daph said that warm evening when the wistaria was out, big grapey lumps of it all dark round Daph's mother's verandah, as if it was down deep south, old Virginia or somewhere, and they had rocked and rocked and fanned themselves and talked at the violet sky. 'Cowardly?' Daph had said. 'Not you. It's your commonsense coming to rescue the romance in you. Because, Marjorie, you're a great dreamer, if on pretty usual lines. I know for a fact— I've heard you talk—that you'd vaguely like to have something to do with say a jewel robbery, or say a bit of smart smuggling in a Mediterranean speed-boat. Right?'

And she had had to admit it, silly as it sounded in cold blood.

Daph had gone on: 'It's not the money with you, nothing as practical as that—you just see yourself in fast cars and smooth launches, among smartly dressed people who never lunch but rise in the late afternoon, having spent the day in bed with one another, and then spend the night talking in short sharp sentences, in small smart clubs, with downdrawn mouths and lowered eyelids. Right?'

Daph could be so rude, breathlessly rude. But she had been dead right.

'And what happens when it comes your way?' Daph had asked. 'With that chemmy party they asked you to drink around at, because of your wild good looks and youth? Chemin-de-fer so-called—off with your chemmy more like. Well, quite rightly you foresaw a *blue-uniformed figure* popping up in every door, and the fan-light too I bet, and my sensible innocent sweet, you never went. Where did you go instead?'

Sandra had had to sigh: 'Home.'

And Daph said: 'Home to Mummy and Sydenham and the mauve glazed tiles you rant on about so. Give you no fireplace at all and a lampstand made of a dozen dunces caps and you'd sigh for the lovely contemporariness of it. But you don't wear a dunce's cap yourself, darling. Except when you call yourself a coward.

'Look at your men. Look at the close shaves you've told me about—but what brought you through, what made you stop? You call it fear, I call it conscience—a nicer name for fear? You've been brought up strictly and carefully, and landed with a load of morality on your hands. Be thankful for it. You're a good girl who wants to be bad, and your fear's just a form of goodness.'

Daph passed a bit over her head with that one. So she had spoken quite sharply:

'Well, I don't see that the girls who've—who've done it seem to change much.'

35

'Don't you believe it,' Daph said. 'Men know, there's something about the eyes, they say.'

But Daph wouldn't say what, she said men even couldn't properly describe it. But how awful it sounded, like a brand, so that they all knew! Bun would have known! And yet that she couldn't imagine, Bun knowing a thing like that, he was too steady. No, it was more a man like Nevile Wrasse who'd be up to such tricks. And Daph had said: 'But the girl knows too, all right. It's funny, you're both proud and ashamed at the same time. You like yourself, secretly, and yet you look down on yourself a bit. And it complicates life horribly. Not having the help of a set line to draw.

'And *another* thing, my girl,' Daph had said— but what were those men saying, what on earth had Hearst just said?

'Okayed,' Hearst had been saying, 'but with the nipple properly painted out, right out.'

A copy of Sue Blair's back had come back to him.

'Well, of course,' Mansford said, 'you don't want to offend—'

'Who? I know, the level-eyed British public. But if that was a black woman, there'd be no order to paint it out, none at all. And they fool themselves there's no colour bar.'

'It's about time,' boomed Mavis Cook right across, 'they put up a colour bar in this office, I mean your partition right round you two.'

'There you are,' Mansford smiled gamely, 'Secretary

addresses London and Southern Area Sales Manager. Democracy. I wouldn't give your colour bar much longer.'

Hearst had reddened.

'Hypocrites!' he said. He was a man who got quickly worked up on odd questions, and the odder the better. 'I suppose they wouldn't want their daughters to see. Yet what have their daughters got there but a pair of—'

He saw Sandra watching him and stopped.

'Passed,' he said, putting the folder in his out-tray.

Daughters, daughters, Sandra thought, and looked up at the clock, twenty-five-to-one, with horror. What can I do? Why did Nevile Wrasse pop up in my mind then?

And, as one tries to regain a day-dream, desperately she tried to think herself back to Daphne on that verandah, for Daph gave her strength. What was it ... *another* thing, wasn't Daph saying? Oh, but it was all that about there being more temptation at home with the telly and the newspapers than being out at a café with a poor young man. It was the telly and so on, Daph said, that gave a girl daily visions of diamonds and convertibles and that, whatever moral message they liked to tag on the end. But wasn't there something more?

Suddenly she burst out laughing. Of course, Daph had begun imitating a preacher:

'Martyrs to transport, that's what we girls are. Once upon a time it was, Would you like to take a walk? Now it's, Get into the car. And we do—it's the only way home. Oh, the battles between the gears! Gaily each time we enter, with our hearts in our hands—and leave with them in our mouths.' And it's worse now the gears are up on the wheel.'

Laughing back, Sandra put herself in a good mood, and typing Yours faithfully to her last letter of the year thought of Nevile Wrasse's low white transport, but with little sense of martyrdom.

'Miss Lee, Miss *Lee*—Sandra!' Ralph Mansford was brandishing the telephone receiver at her.

'No! No!' she squealed without making a sound, gesturing it away with arms waving wide, for she knew it must be Bun.

Mansford off-balance spoke to the receiver:

'No, I'm afraid no news yet, no—I mean, she's out.'

He listened then, saying: 'I don't know when she'll be back . . . sorry, this line *must* be cleared, goodbye.'

'A Mr Stanbetter,' he said, 'called himself Bun.'

Sandra thought, that's done it, I've denied him twice now, when's the cock going to crow? At lunch with Nevile?

But over this, with true sympathy, she said to Mansford:

'Oh dear, I'm sorry, Ralph. And you expecting—I mean a phone-call.'

Mansford sucked air through his teeth in a kind of smile:

'That chap was having a baby too, by the sound of it.'

'Well, he's not having this one,' she parried.

And then once more there was silence but for the

belling and chuttering and crinkling and the no-sound of the red electric second-hand.

She tidied up her desk, feeling freer every minute. It had occurred to her that Bun would think she had gone to lunch early and be back early. So he would ring again. So she could go out to lunch with Nevile this once, and be back early. This once—she thought sadly—perhaps this once and for the last time. She sighed. But as quickly cheered up. She had, after all, arranged to have her cake and eat it. 'Who am I?' she asked herself once again. 'I'm the sensible type.'

'She's the good-time-Charley type,' thought Mansford, 'poor Charley.'

Miss Cook sometimes thought, 'She's the marrying type, underneath all that mess.'

'The near-delinquent type,' dreamed big Hearst, in an imaginative moment, about thirty-six-twenty-two-thirty-six.'

Jill Jenkins had often paused to consider, 'She's the loyal type. I'd trust her anywhere. That child's got her head screwed on all right.'

'Looks a bit screwy,' H. J. had once thought, 'but a solid worker.' And glancing up at her back as she walked off, 'I wonder what it'd be like?'

'Dreamy type,' Monica Naseby had once said, 'airs and graces, crocodile tears, cupboard eyes, silly little cow.'

A big pale-faced office boy on the floor below spent hours thinking, 'Oh, darling Sandra, look at me! Like you did once on the stairs when the lift broke, and I was eating my bun, and you said did it taste good? My own darling, I've got a brand new motor-bike.'

Sue Blair in her Pool thought, 'She's the happy-go-lucky type.'

'I wouldn't have that type near me,' muttered the crabbed old commissionaire below. 'Skin you soon as look at you. Bloody bitch.'

Nevile Wrasse, tuning up his low fast car, thought, 'She's the possible type.'

In their various ways, each was right.

A quarter to one and off to the Powder Room, brisk calves skirting, nearly passing right over the spiderman on the floor, for one was used to him, he came into the category of doctors or bus conductors—and out into the passage. Now Sandra had to pass through the vestibule where an unusually thick carpet, patterned wallpaper, showcases and other decorations flowered for the reception of clients.

This must have been arranged on some premise that an office should look like a home: or, at least, not like an office. But at this time of the year it had a particularly homeless look—for everywhere else, homes and shops, were full of red and green things, holly and Christmas scarlet. Moreover, one corner was furnished with a mounting set-piece of plastic hyacinths bedded on cold grey stones, all lit by a bluish-white fluorescent strip. It was here that Jill caught her up for a quick word before they parted.

'Sandra, I've been thinking,' Jill urged hoarsely confident in her ear, 'you mustn't do it, you mustn't not see Bun. Sandra, he *loves* you,' she said breathless, 'have a heart!'

The hyacinths stared down waxily, more real than rea hyacinths. They were set in a pattern of pink, pale blue, and white, colours of a faded Union Jack. The fluorescent strip lighting revealed them like a flash of livid lightning on a cold spring evening, but worse, for this was a flash that stayed. It always made Sandra sad, it reminded her of the worst evenings at home, in the tidied house in the freezing useless light evenings.

She felt the cold poignancy of spring and allowed a touch of drama to twist down the corners of her lips:

'Have a heart? Maybe it's because my heart is beating too fast,' she said slowly.

As she said it, she could not think what it could mean. But it was the kind of thing Daph might have said—and that was another thing, she often found herself playing the Daph to Jill.

Jill always smelled lightly of cucumbers. It was a cheap lily-of-the-valley scent she used. Now this smell seemed to grow stronger as hotly she bridled:

'But Sandra, all you've said about him and you! How he's part of you, you two always together, grown up together.'

Jill, conscience, hyacinths, all these pressures made her flare. She hit on the first thing she remembered.

'You don't know what he said this morning! He said something a nice girl doesn't talk of. Let alone a man. I don't know what's come over him lately.'

'Childer mine, you'll feel different tomorrow, I know you will. Only then it'll be too late.'

Sandra twisted her smile again, and stared Jill knowingly in the eyes.

'If I stay here much longer I'll be late for Nevile Wrasse—I'm lunching with him.'

'Nevile Wrasse!'

Jill's liquid blue eyes, that always seemed full of water and on the point of tears, brimmed as if to burst.

Sandra shrugged.

'He said he'd wait at the parking meter till quarter past.'

'Oh, Marge, don't go. This is your whole life!'

'Which I'm not going to start off by being spoken to, so there,' and she brushed passed Jill to the Red Hell, whisked up her coat, and left for Nevile's parking meter without another word.

'This'll end in tears,' thought Jill. 'I've never, never seen her not do her face before.'

III

SHE held her coat hard across her spot as she walked to where Nevile Wrasse's low fast car waited.

Nevile sat waiting at the wheel, one arm casually leant out over the side. He was a sharp-beaked young man, with black eyebrows that grew together. The open white car, his sporting fur-collared coat, and a shaft of sunshine made a smart holidayish picture against the business-day traffic all about.

As she walked towards him, his eyes might have twinkled had they been properly visible. But they were small and black, and set in what sometimes seemed two little funnels of bone going back into the brain. He had a reddish skin. He could have been either Welsh or a much-anglicised Jew.

'Ciao, signora!' he smiled as she came up.

She was blinking her green lid-shafts in the sudden sunlight, her mouth smiling downwards in sophisticated deprecation. In return Nevile's eyes inwardly blazed, fixed on her. Not Jewish then, for they would have moved to see also what was happening to either side: this was a Celt, full of the shiftiness that stares straight at you.

She settled herself; and as they drove off, watched by that big pale office boy who had compulsively followed her at a despairing distance, she felt the lovely onrush of escape in the open car driving West-Endwards out of the commercial quarter.

She felt, too, a certain secret thrill to be with Nevile

Wrasse of all people—for Nevile's family lived at the Big House in her district. It was a huge Victorian mansion still standing within walled grounds, a squire's hall among smaller red roofs since built round it. Even now, the Wrasses still commanded something of a squire's social eminence. Despite the fact that at some muddled moment in the 'twenties the house had been renamed Kia-ora Grange, most families about were proud to jockey themselves in through the big-balled gates, into the panelled and winter-gardened approval of 'The Old Lady' and her Lanchester landaulette.

But not the Lees, modern and free. Sandra had happened quite by chance to meet Nevile at a dance at a nearby roadhouse only a week before. Nevile lived in London, he only visited the Sydenham house. He had wandered into the dance from an hour's boredom, had found Sandra, danced with her, fought with her in his car home. His progress in the car had been enough for him to smell success in the not far future, and he had telephoned her once or twice since. She had been busy: she liked to be straight about previous engagements. So this was only their second meeting.

But the slight intimacy in the car after the dance had the effect of estranging them. Now, for want of something to say, she found herself saying:

'God, what a morning it's been.'

Nevile Wrasse was on her like a hawk.

'What happened?' he shot. He was a determined good-listener.

She could not say, and quickly searched:

'Oh, finishing up for the year.'

And added vaguely, 'And preparing for this ghastly office Do we have. And ruining my dress with this spot. How I'll ever enter the Buttery I *don't* know. I'll sink through the floor! I'd have got me a new frock, but there was no time.'

A quick computation clicked in Wrasse's mind. He thought of her coming party and how people in offices at such a time drink too much. Afterwards should be a rewarding opportunity for a date with her. So that this was the time to make certain of a date, a time when a little extra trouble might be taken.

'We'll go to Antonescu's Beautique,' he said. 'It's not far. We've time.'

'What?'

He knew this would frighten her. She would have kept him waiting while she bought a dress, had she had the money to do so.

'For a quick dress,' he said vaguely.

'Oh, you know really, I don't think it's—'

'Sandra mia, don't be a bore.'

'I *beg* your pardon?'

All his teeth flashed:

'Don't be a bore, Sandra. If you want a dress you shall have a dress. It's on me! I've got you cornered, it's Christmas and you can't refuse a present—'

'Oh, Nevile, you *can't*.'

'—even from a dark stranger.'

'No, but. Really, but.'

In the Beautique she was served by a drab-dressed lady

bright with professional patience, whose sighs of sympathy suggested she had known Sandra all her life. Nevertheless Sandra resisted all temptation and decided on one of the least expensive dresses.

'Will madam wear it away?'

'Oh, well, I might just as well.'

Then Nevile strolled casually, carefully away, but only to motion the woman to one side, as Sandra still turned in front of the glass and watched the new blue-green figure, with the usual odd feeling of having seen it all before, although she knew she had not—and she heard Nevile lower his voice but distinctly whisper:

'Put it down to Mrs Wrasse's account.'

She nearly tore the dress straight off. Nevile had never said anything about a wife. How shameful—but you couldn't make a scene in front of the woman; nor take the dress off. After all, you'd said you'd take it.

She gritted her teeth together and went quite white. It was a nice dress. She didn't know what to say. She decided to say nothing, she would freeze.

Outside, Nevile carried her spotted dress wrapped up in a parcel suspended by a loop from one finger, which he held up, elbow into side, in a momentously casual manner which emphasised his broad shoulders. 'They'd better be broad,' she thought, gritting her teeth, yet with a lost feeling.

They entered the Buttery. The management had speckled it with bits of holly in sea-blue felt: upon these leaves, silver robins with black breasts opened their beaks in voiceless song.

Sandra made her way through the tables elegantly, and in a blur of new worry. Was it for her to speak out?

On the first fiery cold rinse of dry martini she said abruptly:

'You never told me you were married, Nevile.'

For a second he was off-balance.

'Whatever gave you that idea?'

Sandra lowered her lids, now in the soft Buttery light no longer too green, to her new dress—but quickly looked away. A present from an interested man was bad enough; but from an interested *married* man!

'It's none of my business,' she said casually among the food-flared, scented, birdlike chatter around, 'but you did say at the Beautique to put it down to Mrs Wrasse's account. Perhaps I shouldn't have heard.'

Nevile smiled thoughtfully and sipped his martini. Then nodded, almost to himself, and said softly:

'Mum's the word.'

Conspiracy! She felt insulted. It made her feel a kept woman. A second later this gave way to a sense of wonderful warmth. Wasn't she wicked and didn't she not care? But Golly—what if his wife walked in now! She popped a number of almonds too quickly into her mouth, and one went right down. She choked coughing.

'Mum's the word—my old mum,' Nevile was saying.

And as she came to she heard: 'Mother sometimes asks me to get her stockings and things there. They know me. Shall we go straight in—or, I don't suppose you'd like another martini?'

'Yes,' she said.

'Go in, you mean?' he asked eagerly, rising.

She had to follow him. The dress began to ruck up in the small of her back. It was always the same, it felt fine in the shop—but afterwards, oh! Now when she sat down it seemed to jib up in the middle, she had to pull her stomach in—how could you eat and pull your stomach in at the same time?

She pretended to read the huge menu card with the French words. This abrupt descent from the wicked had only brought to mind the Time She Got Drunk, and the Man with the Wig. She shuddered.

'O what does all this mean?' She said of the menu, reduced to honesty. 'You choose, Squire.'

Calling him 'Squire' revived another honest moment, when she had told him of all the respect the Wrasses commanded in their parish. They had laughed, worldlily. But afterwards she had regretted it because even for her a Wrasse would never be quite without awe, and, as the night of the dance had proved, even carried near-seignorial rights.

Wrasse ordered oysters, because he had heard of their peculiar potencies, and then a Porterhouse steak for two, because one of his techniques was to order *shared* food, to cut from the same was like sharing a double bed. As he ate, his eyes kept shifting between the black-flared glistening steak and her smooth-skinned arm. Appetite begot appetite—and carefully he put his suggestion for a meeting early that evening.

'We could dance,' he said, and spreading the idea, 'or listen to some records.'

She had raised a glass of Burgundy to her lips. But stopped it there, suspicious:

'Where?' she asked.

He caught it instantly, and pretended:

'Oh, at that club, what's it called. You know.'

She sipped at her glass. 'Love to,' she said. My God, what have I said? What about Bun?

'Then could we meet at my flat at about half-six?'

'But why there—why not—'

'Trouble is,' he said slowly, 'I've got to wait in for a long-distance call.'

'Oh.'

'I wouldn't want to keep you hanging about.'

'You're thoughtful, Nevile, very thoughtful.'

'Then you don't mind?'

Just then she caught sight of half of a woman in a dress either the same or similar to hers sitting right across the room. She craned her neck to see. A waiter came in the way. She nodded absently to Nevile.

'All right,' she murmured.

Another waiter joined the first. It was infuriating. And Nevile was newly demanding attention. He had been quick to start a new topic in case she changed her mind.

'And what,' he was saying, 'does it feel like to be free after all these months cooped up in Allasol? I mean, you're with all those people you see day after day, and suddenly they're gone, and you're all alone.'

'Hurr,' she mouthed, winding from eyes to brain, 'all alone? What on earth do you mean? I'm never—oh, glad,' she said.

'Okay, signora, I grant you your freedom,' he said. 'But is there not a kind of, well, a psychological loss which leaves you like a prisoner without your rat?'

'Without my rat?'

'Meaning no disrespect, I'm on the side of freedom, as you know,' insisted Nevile, now at the water-ice stage of cool digestive reflection, 'and what it could be like cooped up with the same people all the year I don't know.'

Wrasse prized his own freedom. He was acting as Outer London traveller in smoking accessories—Mrs Wrasse's money came from tobacco retail. His freedom was to spend ten hours a day battling through metro-politan traffic or speeding with taut eyes along motorways to visit an unvarying round of the same clients.

'It's funny you say that,' Sandra replied, 'because only this morning I was looking at them all, that is the ones near me, for there are more than seventy at Allasol all told. And I was thinking I don't really know *anything* about them. That is, I do in one way—I mean, I know what they seem to be in the office, but is that really them? Is that their real them?'

'I know what you mean,' Nevile nodded wisely.

The waiters had now wheeled a trolley piled with puddings in the way of that woman in the dress. She gave up. Besides, she wanted to tell this.

'But you *don't*,' she said eagerly, and her eyes opened and the defensive mask fell away, she looked suddenly twice as pretty. 'You don't. It came over me quite sud-denly. I thought—they all have mantelpieces in their lounges, and on all their mantelpieces they have put their different things, vases and clocks and that, and I don't know a thing about them! It sounds silly, but their mantelpieces made them seem suddenly all like foreigners. Mind you, I could guess at *some*. Monica Naseby's, for instance.'

Wrasse continued carefully smoking and playing the good listener. She really is a bit of a smasher, he thought.

'Oh?' he said. 'Really?'

'A most superior modern clock all squares and no hands. And some other blasted thing nobody's ever seen before.'

'What's that?'

'I don't know. Nobody could know. A stuffed owl standing on its head. A huge great daffodil covered with postage stamps. I don't know.'

'Stamps?' said Neville uneasy.

'*She's* not contemporary, not her. The great Miss Naseby's one step ahead. *She* must have what everyone else's going to get in six month's time. You should hear her arguing with young Mark Deane—he's our P.R.M., Public Relations Manager, boss's nephew—to change how he sets up the office dee-cor. Monica says its out-of-date—passy. But Mark says it's meant like that, his style is "old contemporary", he says, to please the provincial clients and that, who've just got there.'

'I see what you mean,' said Nevile.

'Well, that's *her* mantelpiece. Now there's Mavis Cook's, she's H. J. the boss's secretary, and if anyone resents Monica it's Mavis. Mavis is the old trusty of the firm, and Monica's an upstart, Monny came later as H. J.'s personal assistant, cutting Mavis out, and everyone knows Mavis has a crush on H. J.'

As she talked on, warming up, Nevile Wrasse began to eat her again. Playing the listener, it was nevertheless difficult to stare all the time into her eyes—so he let his own travel all over her torso and her arms, round the queer-cut halo of hair, in and out the creases in the pancake of her face. But he snapped them back now and then to look piercingly sincere, and to nod. 'Wonder how far she'll go?' he thought. 'Better get some gin in.'

'Well, Mavis's mantelpiece you almost could tell—because she's more or less brought it to the office. What I mean is, she's more or less furnished her little corner all around her with personal odds and ends and thingummies.'

'Half a bottle'll do,' thought Nevile. 'Keep off it myself. Don't want to gum the works.'

'She's got her biscuits in a tin, Scotchy looking, and her calendar, her wool and her library book. There's a hanger for an extra cardigan, and a little plaster doggie and even her poker-work notice that says *Don't pick it*. The homely type, but no home of her own, poor thing, only a bedsitter. Home's the office, and she's loyal to the backbone.

'Loyalty's a great thing,' said Nevile gravely, frowning his joined black eyebrows closer together. 'Loyalty and trust, deep down there in your heart.'

His face opened out in a mask of innocence. He looked as if he were praying or had seen a distant vision.

'Yes, sir?' said a waiter, mistaking this look for an appeal for help. 'Would you like a liqueur?'

'No,' Nevile began, but had to add to Sandra: 'I suppose you wouldn't like a liqueur?'

'Yes,' Sandra said, her mind on her mantelpieces.

Nevile frowned.

'Then we'll have something rather special,' he said. 'Two crème de cacaos,' he told the waiter, knowing these to be cheaper. 'And sod you for interfering,' he added under his breath.

'Then there's Ralph Mansford's,' she continued, 'you can soon get *his* off your mind—a silver-framed photograph of his wife and another of the wedding. And a few pipes and a pair of slippers.'

'On the chimney-piece?' suddenly snapped Wrasse, still annoyed at those liqueurs. 'You might say I'm in the business of supplying for chimney-pieces—anything from a Toby Jug with your Aunt's first name on it to a Tower Bridge Cigarette and Music Box—but I've never heard of slippers. You've slippered up there!'

'What?' said Sandra.

'Slippered' laughed Nevile nervously, his red and black face opening lines of little white teeth. He looked like a ventriloquist's dummy crossed with a crow.

Sandra said sharply: 'Ralph Mansford's a much-married father-to-be. Not that what he may be no better than he should, if the truth were told,' she added darkly of all men.

And Nevile's hand rich with dark hair instantly grasped hers on the white tablecloth, he urged his face forward fatherly, protective.

'Not with you?' he asked. 'This chap's not been pestering, has he, because if he *has*, I'll . . .'

He felt her flinch within his claw. He saw he had made a mistake. He removed it, though slowly, drawing his last finger lightly across hers, soft as a butterfly kiss.

'Oh no, no, no, not Ralph,' she said shaking her head, when suddenly a flare-dish blinded up bright as a photographer's flash, shivering all her mantelpieces to fragments—and at the same time that woman in the dress rose so that at last she could see. Nevile was saying '. . . out to Ruislip and back by six, I can be waiting at the flat from six on . . .' and the woman came nearer and she saw the dress was the same exactly as hers!

Though she had chosen it, fury flashed up at Nevile. A party at the next table suddenly laughed loud like a thunderclap.

'Ruislip?' she said, curling her lip.

'Well, why not? I've got my retailers, haven't I?'

But it was *not* the same dress! It was cheap compared with hers! In a flash she took in the stitching and hem-line and much else—including the look on the woman's face as she saw Sandra—and turned again to Nevile bright with pleasure, to this dark well-dressed man who had bought her this dress, dark-eyed Nevile with whom she had a date at half-six, at his flat.

'But I *like* Ruislip,' she said warmly.

Up down, up down, one moment against Ruislip, the next moment for it—what are they made of? But Nevile smiled gratefully, as at a great favour granted.

Then he paid the bill; and frowned as he saw how much difference a couple of liqueurs made—much more than they made to her, he thought, and made a mental note to go as far as a whole bottle of gin.

It was half-past two when they rose in the emptying Buttery. Waiters were flicking at last crumbs on bare white tablecloths, bluish smoke hung about lonely. A wire-haired young under-waiter bowed as she passed. Beings of another world, she thought, handsome as Gods but as untouchable—then rebuked herself at this, and smiled sincere benevolence at the young man. At the same time she rested her hand on Nevile Wrasse's arm.

But a moment later out of the warmth of soft carpets and shaded yellow light, she saw her face in a sudden sad daylit mirror, fussed it quickly with a passing puff—and was weighed with remorse at the sacrifice of her youth. Had it to be? Though through her make-up Nevile could discern little expression, her eyes were then bruised and gently melancholy.

'See you at half-six, then?' he said. 'I've got to look sharp now.'

She nodded slowly.

But his eyes were already working along the street to judge his parking place, her bus. She had thanked him, casually, inside the restaurant. But now she repeated it:

'Thank you, really, ever so much, Nevile. For lunch, and for the dress. Really, thank you ever so much indeed.' In this emphasis she both expressed and escaped obligation.

'Cheeroh,' grinned Nevile, trying his best to look frank.

She then saw he still held the parcel of her old dress. He said with a smile:

'I'll put it in the car. You don't want to carry it all the way to the office and back to the flat, do you?'

Before she could think of anything to say he was striding off, almost at a run.

IV

ON the bus her thoughts went to Bun.
How could she have been so heartless? In the soft
rich glitter of the restaurant, it had come so easily. Now
she was alone again, back among ordinary things, wedged
small in a window seat with a big-coated man pressing
against her and pretending to read his paper and slanting
his eye on her. She felt small and afraid.

And that parcel! All very well to agree to a date—but
to have one's escape route blocked was another matter.
Escape route? Now that's a bit better, she thought—that
means I mightn't have gone after all. Oh, what's a dress?
she thought angrily. A dress, the answer was.

It was much later now than she had planned, but there
was still time to phone Bun. At the same time, there was
time running out for other things—for what? The bus-
gears grinding, voices arguing, the conductor's bell and
his weary witty call—Bun, she thought, dear Bun, I'm not
being fair to him. He's always been fair and good to me.
How can I do this to him? But I haven't done anything
yet—I'm my own mistress, aren't I?

Mistress of your thoughts, though? You know you've
deceived him by thinking of it. And by luxuriating in a
car and a lunch and a dress with a young man you know
is fairly attractive. And with whom in a car after a dance
—but that must be forgotten. Not to be thought of. A
slip. Gone, past, compartmented off in the night and in

its own darkness. Also, in the last resort it could be excused under the heading 'transport'.

Yet it had been an inglorious scuffle—the most she could now remember was fear. And, of course, a sense of failure. Successful sin can be conveniently forgotten: failure hangs about forever.

The man sitting next to her pressed himself harder. She felt his eyes. She twisted her neck away to look hard out of the window. Tops of people hurrying against the brown pavements, a girl with a blue overnight air-bag full of parcels—'I've been to Australia!' it seemed to squeak. Sandra only envied her. And, damn this old beast, she was getting a crick in her neck. She gave an exasperated loud sigh, pulling her coat to herself markedly, and looked round at him with a quick frown. He was quicker, his eyes burrowing into the news.

She gave a louder snort, and turned this against Bun. His nice kind eyes, his love she could trust. But can I? she thought irritated. You wouldn't put it past any man! Yet—I can't *see* it of Bun, not him. When he looks at me that way—both lost and found at the same time. But who on earth can ever tell?

And me and Nevile—really, it's Christmas, it's not like any time, everybody's a bit crazy, it's like something taking place as it were not in this world but in a bubble, right inside a tinsel bubble . . . anyway, Bun'll never know, and thank God, here's my stop.

She stepped on the man's foot and brushed his paper roughly as she passed him to get off. This made her feel a little better. Opposite the stop was a shop labelled

Discerie, full of record sleeves. She paused to admire the magic oily gloss of these strangely coloured covers. How beautifully they did them, how rich they were, much richer than a mouldy old bookshop. They oozed golden wealth, rich throb and thrum of music mellowed to massage the nerves, to float the soul away . . . and there was Don Terry's *Yours, Yours*. In a lilac suit against a giant olive and orange candelabra, Don poised his thin silver soprano saxophone to make a magician's wand, all on thick glossed paper you could bite into with your teeth.

'Yours,' she hummed softly, 'yours . . .'

And record players for sale, plastic pick-ups, black and gold and red transistor sets as shining and secret as jewel boxes . . . in spite of the cold she quietly opened her coat and inspected her new dress darkly mirrored in plate-glass among these beautiful luxurious things, a dark smart figure, she reflected, bound for . . . where? . . . and again a kind of empty feeling in her stomach, fear of foolishness, started inside. Then the figure with its smart extraordinary shapes of coat shoulder and hair answered her:

'You owe it to yourself.'

In an underground Sherry Bar, in an alcove behind a pillar, Godfrey Deane and Monica Naseby sat together, knees touching, and holding hands.

'Sod oils! Pickled Fleshers!' Deane was saying, 'you should read it. Crust Skivers! And over everything, the menace of the leather-loving Warble Fly! What does it all mean? How can I learn a new trade? I'm tired out already.'

'Darling,' she laughed, 'you've only been at that Leather Trades Journal again. Chin up! Quite decided not to sell the new company?'

Deane's chin jutted firmly, a rock of commerce:

'We'll keep it,' he snapped. 'On the one hand, here's this leather concern fallen into our laps: on the other, we've got to expand. Diversify. No organisation keeps to one line of product these days. Your ice-cream manufacturer makes golf-balls, your ship-builder has his knitwear on the side. The old complementary idea's finished—a Sheffield cutler palling up with a sticking-plaster concern. That sort of thing's out. You've got to provide against a rainy day. Provide mushroom cover.'

'Mushroom?' she asked.

His far-seeing expression dropped away, he looked blankly at her, then twinkled.

'Did I say that?' he said. 'The truth is, this whole business is sending me off my nut. I'm tired out.'

She looked at him anxiously, but with a kind of braveness. It was a hopeless situation. He inextricably married, she lost in love with him. And she was past thirty. Their affair had already lasted a year.

'It's nearly zero hour,' she said, 'you're in for staff trouble before you're much—' but she stopped at that word.

He fingered the plate in front, pushed a radish-top against cheese-rind.

'I saw Miss Lee this morning, and I must say she took the reduced Message very well.'

'Probably didn't penetrate. Bone from the neck up.'

'Oh? I don't agree quite. I've been watching that girl—'

'Godfrey Puss!' She made a naughty scowlface.

'No, it's funny, but one moment she's bright as a button, says something really imaginative and constructive—and the next, well, as dumb as they're made.'

She laughed, her big tongue curled luscious over little lower teeth.

'But aren't you describing us all, Pussy dear?'

He smiled and leaned towards her.

'Monica,' he said, loving.

She murmured: 'Godfrey.' And they looked at each other quietly for a while, nothing more to say.

Presently he said: 'Well, I expect she'll be off married soon. They all do. What's the use of taking an interest in them.'

She took her hand away, and looked up at the clock.

'Time,' she said, and finished her port.

Then, quietly: 'Godfrey, you are staying up tonight, aren't you?'

He placed money in the plate, and put out his lower lip.

'Yes,' he said, doubtfully. 'Though I really shouldn't—'

'Oh, darling!'

'—all this decorating. Christmas is such a family business.'

'But Godfrey, this is *our* part of Christmas.'

'Yes,' he said blankly. And then smiled at her, 'Yes, it is.'

Sandra was nearly knocked over by sudden singing passers-by.

'Pardong, mamzel!' a man shouted as he was swept away arm-in-arm with others full of the first Christmas drinks.

'Good King Wencelas, look out!' another shouted, seeing how fiercely she was painted. But Sandra, her hair knocked awry, only waved to them and laughed.

The bump cheered her. They were having fun. My, she thought, they've started early. And then, noticing how dark the afternoon had become, she began to hurry.

The winter streets were chilly and damp, buses had their lights on early and hissed past with yellow windows and a sense of going home to tea. She hurried faster among people carrying parcels, and occasional groups lurching and singing like parts of a football crowd wandered into this drab commercial quarter.

Down a side street a butcher's bulged with big naked birds. All the shops were red and green and tinselled. Everyone else seemed to be having Christmas, she was having only trouble, secrets, decisions. Only she left out of the fun. It was a familiar depression, carried along since childhood and children's parties. And now she thought of all the millions in London, of the West End strung with lanterns and reindeer and coloured angels, and of all the trains that evening which would deliver to the suburbs a new cock-eyed kind of clerk, and flushed girls laden with parcels and hiccups.

But not for me, she thought. Although she was in fact bound for a party, she felt that only other people had parties. That was how this feeling always took her. She now yearned for Christmas, for everything to do with it, for aching feet and cards winking all over the room, for wild student-postmen who looked as if they would throw away the letters and parcels fed-up, for the loosening of purses and the bells and the pagan evergreen every-where, the port and jelly and gravy-tasting bright light that dazzled the middle of dark December, the holy roof of a child's voice singing alone in church; alone but accompanied by so much, not alone like her, with only the clouds of low January ahead.

She skirted the first laughing sputter of vomit on the pavement. 'Oh, how I hate myself,' she said aloud. 'Oh my darling Bun, where are you?'

Bun Stanbetter stood in the surgery of the Tropical Disease Centre with one arm bared to the shoulder, and ground his teeth.

'You married?' asked the doctor, filling a syringe.

'No,' Bun said.

'Just as well.'

Bun said: 'Just as well what?'

'Just as well not,' the doctor said. 'You never know with women out there.'

Bun gritted harder on his teeth. The day and every-thing had been too much.

'I am shortly to be married,' he said with emphasis. 'And what, anyway, do you mean?'

'Hm,' the doctor said, and scrubbed at his arm with spirit.

Since the doctor was about to pierce him, Bun said, more gently:

'You mean, I suppose, that some don't stand up to it as well as others.'

The doctor stuck the needle in.

'Yes,' he said, 'that's about what I mean.'

He dabbed the wound, tossed the arm away and said jovially, reassuring, finished:

'But some do, you know, oh yes, some do. Not to worry. Some do.'

Bun put on his coat and went over to where the doctor consulted his book about final injections. How much longer, he sighed to himself. Bun was a tall man with big ears and a forelock of fair hair tousling over his forehead. His long good-looking face was pink and white, boney and smooth—in a manly way he had something of the look of an immense girl, a big scrubbed strapper from the shires, and his voice was suitably deep.

As the doctor pencilled at his book Bun suddenly thought: 'He couldn't have meant that, could he? It couldn't be that unhealthy for her, could it?'

He was about to ask the doctor—when he suddenly felt helpless. What was the use? First she would come, then she wouldn't. He hated feeling helpless. Why couldn't she make up her mind? Well, he supposed, changing seemed to be a woman's privilege, taken all in all.

He pressed his lips together. Patience, he said, brute patience. I'll wear her out in the end.

'Is there a phone about, Doctor?' he asked.

Jill Jenkins was saying to the man in the Gifts Department:

'But I want one without adjustable howdah.'

The man raised his eyes above her head, and said quietly:

'If you'd have come earlier, madam, you could have had one without. We've only these left.'

Jill bit her lip. She looked up and down the counter, all over the boxes behind:

'You see, my friend's going to Sarawak and I suddenly sort of thought, when I saw your elephants, I'll give her an elephant. An elephant's just the thing. She's going to be married, you see.'

'Quite, madam. But surely the lady would like one with adjustable howdah just as well? That is, even better?'

Jill crinkled her mouth up into a baby-crying face, thinking this cute but making herself look exceedingly ugly.

'But they're not so—sort of elephanty. Not with the adjustable thingummies.'

'Then I'm afraid we must disappoint you, madam.'

'Are you sure there's not just one little one hiding somewhere? I was in here on the Tuesday, or was it the Wednesday, no the Tuesday, and I saw *lots*.'

The man tried to smile:

'We've had quite a run on them without the adjustable, madam.'

Jill leaned forward confidentially:

'As a matter of fact, she might not get married after all. So then it wouldn't matter so much, would it? Actually?'

'No.'

'We're getting our bonus cut in half today so I don't think I could afford the adjustable, not even if I wanted one. Of course, she's the nervous type, sort of holds herself in. It's a big decision in a woman's life. You've got to think of it that way. I don't suppose you'd have just one more wee tiny look, would you?'

The man had had a week of it. He leaned forward over the counter, spread his hands out to grip it and himself, and addressed Jill quietly and emphatically, but with jaw quivering:

'My mum,' he said, 'was one of eight and she went out to work at sixteen cleaning. Her old man was on the dole, and she worked twelve hours a day when she was your age and went hungry too with all the kids to feed and *she* wouldn't have worried her guts out and everybody else's as to if her elephant had adjustable howdah or not adjustable howdah, my mum would have had no elephant *at all*. Not on the Tuesday nor the Wednesday nor any day of the week. My Mum would have been pleased with ANY BLOODY ELEPHANT,' he shouted.

Jill's face crumpled again, but this time of its own accord.

The man lowered his voice, stood back, and said coldly:

'In any case, madam, there are no elephants in Sarawak.'

Flushed and young in the winter air, dressed to kill and bouncing on her high heels as she passed plain women and faded women and fading women who envied her,

66

Sandra only said to herself: 'Why am I so wretched? Why do I hold in so? What's wrong with me?'

A clock put the time at nearly five minutes to three. 'And now this party! I'll ring Bun the moment I get in.'

An abrupt noise of singing, as if a loud radio-van was passing—a pub door had swung open and was now held wide by Christmas drinkers almost tumbled out by the crowd inside. She stopped dead. It was like suddenly looking into an electric night from day, carnival night with lights blazing and packed faces swaying and singing. You could hardly see the streamers for the smoke. Mackintoshes, duffle-coats, glasses, beer, moustaches, red lips. Packed clerks with pale faces roared and drank like giants, flushed typists brimming with crème de menthe and Cherry Heering shrieked with laughter, purse-free old men sweated red-faced, wedged in a beery heaven, happy as lark-puddings.

Sandra stood on the cold pavement and gazed in not like the poor child left out, for a millionaire could not have found room inside—they were packed closer than the rush-hour whose temporary cessation they celebrated —she simply gazed in wonder.

She did not see Ralph Mansford and Hearst wedged between glee-singing chartered accountants and a pin-table, nobody could have.

Ralph was saying for the fifth time, after as many glasses: 'I ought not to be here. I ought to be there.'

Hearst stolidly chewed a mint humbug:

'We've just been there,' he said, 'you ass. Have a drop more of the old twilight sleep.'

'I won't say no. You've never been through this, old man?'

'I was the victim of an early Change. Shortly afterwards she left me for the columbarium.'

'Oh, I say—no idea—I am sorry.'

'Never been happier in my life,' Hearst said glumly. 'It was like a hundred Margates wrapped in one.'

'Oh. Didn't get on, eh?'

'Not badly. She was a very decent sort. Only—'

'Then why?'

'Never could put my finger on it. Only. That's about it. Only.' He popped another humbug into his mouth. 'These don't half tug your lower lot about,' he said. 'She used to knit for hours. I used to say it kept her mind occupied while she talked.'

'They don't knit like that nowadays.'

Hearst said: 'That was a joke.'

'Oh.'

They were pressed closer together. Wet beer, mackintoshes—it was like sheltering from a rainstorm.

'Anyway, they don't,' said Ralph. 'Not like your Mavis. What do they do all the time, what do they think of?'

'Less of the *my* Mavis. Listen to records, that's what they do. And when they're not listening to records they're remembering listening to records. Take a kid like Sandra.'

'Oh, she's a decent enough little thing.'

'Yes, but what is she interested in—but records, and boys, and what she looks like? And cars.'

'Excuse me, old man, is that my hand holding your glass?'

'Couldn't say. Well, I suppose it's us that give it them. Pump it down their throats all the time, ads, telly.'

'Too much money in their pockets, that's what.'

'We give them that, too' Ralph said. 'We want a hundred thousand more cream cakes made, so we fill the factories with them and pay them well. Else no cream cakes. Bob's your uncle.'

'Not enough discipline in the home,' Hearst said.

'You try and control 'em with ten quid in their pockets. Besides, old man, they're what we live off. Where would Allasol be without the affluent teenager? Let's get out of here—got an axe?'

They began forcing their way out through packed bodies.

'Still,' Hearst said over a shoulder, 'I suppose we had our own crazes. And I must say about that girl, even if she does look like the bloody Queen of Sheba (no not you, madam) she'll always do you a thumping good turn.'

Ralph yelled: 'Offered to sit in by the telephone for me yesterday lunch. And run and find me if.'

'Oh, they're human. (Yes sir, I know it's your beer.) Treats that blasted office cat like a real prince, too.'

'More than she does her boy friend,' Ralph shouted. 'Lend some weight, Tiny.'

Good Lord, Sandra thought outside—good heavens, is that what it's going to be like this afternoon? And walked on long before the two men managed to punch through the mass-packed mackintoshes into the failing light of day.

The office was still empty. People were still out buying last presents. Typewriters sat by themselves, empty chairs were pushed back, and silence—it reminded Sandra of working late after hours, when you are tempted to look in other people's drawers, or sit in their chairs for a few moments.

She went straight over to her own desk and pulled out a big morocco scrap-book from where it lay hidden among rubbers, old lipsticks, a broken compact, hair-pins knotted with paper-clips, cotton-wool and all the rest. She turned the pages to look for Don Terry. Yes, he was there, as she thought, against the candelabra. But the candelabra was red, and he was blue! It was the same photograph, but more cheaply printed. Now was that not interesting? Well.

Her eyes once more licked over the shape of his neck, his sad black eyes, his trick of raising one shoulder. She sighed. Then idly began turning the pages of cuttings from coloured magazines and record-sleeves which with such love and care she had pasted in. A starlet in a wisp of short nightgown kissed a rose in a foggy garden. A gold-gowned German night-club singer led on a leash not salukis but two Shetland ponies. A fresh-faced girl in a romp-suit leapt from cold Essex water, a sky like a pale blue hymn of racket-thwangs behind. Then, surprisingly, a whole page advertisement of gadgets, Kidditents, icing-guns, scoutlamps, aprons saying His and Hers. Followed by Tintern Abbey, in four colours.

By these beautiful glossy things she was profoundly moved. They corresponded to moments of vision. Not anything could go in this book—only special things, which at special moments had made her heart leap. On a simple level—because she knew no other—her sensations were wholly aesthetic and poetic.

Her thoughts went back to Daphne. Daph was one of the very few to whom she had shown her book. Daph had laughed at first.

'Quite the little Victorian,' Daph had said. 'Scrapbook indeed!'

That was where Daph was wrong. She had quite a few friends who loved cutting things out and keeping them, half-secretly indeed. But afterwards Daph had often dawdled over the book. One of the great attractions was 'typing' people. Daph understood that. Seriously and fascinated, they would drink in the effect of ash-grey hair on tanned shoulders, the mysterious look in a pair of blue eyes under black hair.

'I know that type,' Daph would say, 'April rain.'

If you changed your hair-style and make-up, you could quite easily become one of these people. But others you could never become. Yet you liked them as well; for they were types. You knew somebody like them. That was interesting.

Of course, they had their differences. Naturally enough, because it was her book and her choice.

'I don't see what you can see in him,' Daph had said about Don Terry.

She had tried to explain. 'He's so—he's the—' but it was impossible and she would end up merely with: 'He's the soulful type.' Yet it was really the picture which explained everything in such rich tongue-tasting detail.

'And he's the dead opposite to your Bun Stanbetter,' Daph had said, 'explain that one.'

It was certainly a facer. For a moment she had wondered if this could be why she did not melt in Bun's arms. Yet of course she did melt. Only in another sort of way. Knowing someone was very different to dreaming of somebody. 'I expect you can go for all sorts of types,' she had said. And had added, 'Besides, looks aren't everything.' She bit her lip, it sounded so disloyal to Bun. Besides, she did think him good-looking. It was all rather alarming. And Daph had given her such a strange, shrewd look.

A black-eyed blonde with a brown lipstick, dressed only in a corset, sat in a box at the opera. Sandra pored over this scene with the lost addiction of a fetichist, or of a child at a toyshop window, fixed, fixed on one thing only. Underneath, a photograph in colour of a new box-camera said: 'Requires no Know-how.'

And what would Daph have said about this afternoon, and Bun, and Nevile? She remembered her smirking once at some similar predicament.

'Do both,' Daph had said. 'Where there's a woman, there's a way.'

Then she had looked wise. 'The silliest thing that was ever said,' Daph had said, 'is you can't have your cake and eat it. It applies pretty well only to cake, dear. What people are doing every day of their lives is doing three-quarters of what they shouldn't do, and having three-quarters peace of mind left. Add that one up. Twice three-quarters is one and a half, my girl. People are making more cake, that's all.'

Now, in the empty office, she imagined asking Daph about marrying Bun and thus missing things.

'What things?' Daph asked.

'Oh—things. Things I don't even know. I wouldn't miss them if I knew, would I?'

Daph's eyes half closed, she let out a long slow trail of cigarette smoke. She was wearing her brown.

'But you must know, child,' she said.

This was the terrible question. The answers sounded so trivial. Driving fast in a fast car? Meeting strange sophisticated people who would suddenly 'discover' her, make her their mascot? Or that moment of a new dress, when you feel all eyes are on you with approval, gasping eyes— only this time at some fabulous ball. Or travel to foreign parts—but then why not Sarawak with Bun, that was foreign enough. But it was not the same. Or, she thought sadly—just an affair with someone? You couldn't put it as baldly as that, but it was true. Say an affair-plus, then. With an artist, an actor, something new—damn Daph and her questions.

Just then Daph said something rather rotten. She could be quite a bitch.

'Anyhow,' Daph said, 'Bun's no great shakes, if you ask me.'

'I'm not asking you,' she told her straight back, blushing. But she half-suspected this was only Daph's clever way of getting her going. Stimulating, it was called.

'An electrical engineer,' Daph said.

'What's wrong with that?' Sandra answered hotly. 'He's been studying very hard for three years. On very little money.'

'You should know.'

'Another man would go and get a good easy job. But Bun's got an eye to the future, he wants the best job. He's not settling for just anything, not Bun.'

'Lah-di-dah. Best job in sweaty Sarawak among a lot of black people. Heaven knows what you'll catch. Mosquitos big as birds.'

'He's true and he's steady. And he won a rowing cup and he dances like a dream, he's awfully clever too, You should hear the things he says sometimes. And we laugh together. We're real friends, Daph. Remember, it's security too.'

'Security, my love? At your age?'

'He's a man you can trust, you can lean on him, he's true and steady and dependable.'

Daph closed her eyes.

'And are you?' she said.

'Oh, shut up!' said Sandra aloud, quite red, and rose to flounce out of the empty office.

But there had been a noise, a loom of shadow, as someone came to stand behind her. She stopped, her heart jumped, she closed the book quickly.

'Shut up yourself,' a voice said.

But it was only Jill Jenkins.

'My, you gave me a fright! Has Bun phoned?'

'Deep in your old book again,' Jill said, putting down new parcels on her desk.

74

When she saw these, Sandra was suddenly ashamed. She had forgotten to buy Bun his Christmas tobacco. All the rest she had bought, all her list was done but this.

'Then he'll just have to be content with pouch and pipe,' she told herself, removing the blame to him.

'A man's just been rude to me in a shop,' Jill said. 'They're ever so bolshy just now, aren't they? There we were, chatting away sweet as pie, when suddenly he ups and—oh, but I can't tell *you*,' she ended in horror at herself talking of Sandra's lost elephant.

'Why ever not?'

'That would be telling, wouldn't it?' Jill laughed. 'By the way, your Bun's been on again and he says he's going to call at five.'

'Not until then? Where is he?'

'Don't ask me. The switchboard just said he's calling at five.'

'I can't sit by the telephone until then.'

'Not call, silly, they said *call*. Hello, I'm blind, I didn't see the new frock!'

'Call here!' cried Sandra in alarm. 'When we've got the party?' She felt now that something dreadful was to happen. Life was closing in.

Jill Jenkins opened her big watery blue eyes wide, her mouth too.

'It's smashing,' she said, 'I love that greeny-bluey style. I'll give me three guesses who gave you *that*!'

'What'll I ever say when he comes?'

'Give over! You've seen him since he phoned, my

girl, else why the glad rags? I think it's sweet of your Bun to give it you.'

'Bun?'

'You might be married already!'

'Bun give me this?' Sandra's eyes opened, and then narrowed until only green grease and black kohl could be seen, with a slit of dangerous light between.

'Huh,' she said, and slowly.

'Oh, quit acting,' Jill was saying as, just then, an office lad called Bossom, an energetic young man with a long upper lip like a monkey's, came in, bowed, slapped up an out-tray, bowed again, and sang as he went out:

'While shepherds washed their socks one night
In Allasol's nodourless Fresh!'

Sandra's slit eyes turned in surprise on this departing figure.

'Don't worry,' Jill said. 'Nothing to what you'll see in an hour or two—'

But Sandra was not listening, she was only thinking how sad it was to have a guilty secret if you couldn't tell anyone. It suddenly all seemed a sell. What was the good of sinning if nobody knew? Surely it couldn't be worth it for its *own* sake? She turned back to Jill and said very slowly, marking every word:

'This dress was given to me by Nevile Wrasse.'

Jill gurgled in her neck, as if something lovely but horrid, a 50 denier nylon, were throttling her.

'Marge!' she squealed, forgetting herself.

But for once Sandra did not notice this word. She

looked quickly round the office to make sure it was quite empty, and leaned close to Jill:

'And I'll tell you something else Jill Jenkins, that I never told anyone else. Do you remember a boy I went out with a year ago, Andrew by name?'

Jill said breathless: 'Sandra I don't want to hear.'

'Remember? A dark boy with a big head I met at some coffee-bar? So I didn't know him well at all—but suddenly I seemed to get crazy about that boy. And one night I went up to his room he had in Baron's Court. He had some records he wanted me to hear.'

'Oh, Sandra, you didn't know what you were doing!'

Sandra made her mouth droop. 'I knew all right,' she said, 'I said I was crazy, didn't I? But I didn't know all, not by a long shot. Anyhow, we got cosy and he played his records, and then we got cosier, and he asked me to take off my dress. I said no, but well—you know how it is?'

'No,' Jill said too quickly. 'No, no, no I don't.'

Sandra looked at her sharply.

'Anyhow,' she said, 'I did. And d'you know—he went straight out of the room!

'But only into his bathroom, I could hear him. I had a slip on, it was January, and I sat there thinking—Oh, Lord, I've done it now. And then he called, "You do look lovely" and I remember thinking, "He's got hairpin eyes if he can see round the door." And then he came in, my dear, without a stitch on but his short pants.'

'Oh!'

Sandra's mouth-droop lengthened. 'I know what

you're thinking, and I thought about the same. He came towards me, I shrank back—and then quick as lightning he reached down and slipped on my dress!'

'What?'

'Oh, Jill, I didn't know where to look. And then he walked on his toes over to a drawer and took out a big curly wig and put it on and then he—'

Jill Jenkins gasped:

'He was a convert!'

'Pervert, Jill. He was such a goodlooking boy, too. Though he had the biggest hands of any man I've ever seen.'

'Sandra, what did you do?'

'Do?' Sandra gave a small, sarcastic laugh. '*Do?* I had that dress off his back in two ticks, I can tell you.'

Just then Mavis Cook came in with a 'Hello all, my *feet*!'—and Jill was left wondering goodness knows what else went on that night in Baron's Court.

Yet how could Sandra have told her what had then in fact happened, and which she tried hard not to remember —that the man had never once tried to touch her? That he was only interested in how he looked in her dress?

And how she had stood up imperiously to leave—only of course she couldn't leave while he was in her dress, so she had had to chase him round that awful room in it and it was so dreadful because she could not tear it off, not her own dress, and she even had to get round the back of him to get at the zip . . . and then he would turn and titter at her, and then run off again round the table giggling with delight, round and round and round they went . . . it was

78

a nightmare and to think of it now made her go hot and cold and near to tears.

But tears—those were what Andrew had shed when at last she had the dress off him. He had just squatted down and buried his face in his hands and sobbed his heart out. And that was how she had left him.

Humiliating, or sordid, or pathetic—a hateful story. But luckily she had now left Jill with the half-truth and wide-eyed: and this was halfway to believing it herself. She felt a little cheered. And no more could be said because Mavis Cook was established in her corner, arranging her cardigans and scarves and parcels as if for a stay of weeks.

'I'm quite squiffy already,' she called to Sandra and Jill.

'Was that always your intention then Miss Cook?' asked Hearst, his great size suddenly filling the doorway.

'Landsakes, the Sheriff!' cried Miss Cook, 'I had a glass of ginger wine.'

Hearst's eyebrows went up. 'Ginger-your-barmy,' he said.

'I'll ginger-your-barmy you,' twinkled Miss Cook stiffly. 'Christmas comes but once a year,' she added, taking from her big embroidered shopping sack a dark brown bottle with a green label.

Sandra and Jill sighed to each other knowingly, as if to say, 'Those two are off again.' And in came Ralph Mansford with a long lurch.

His handsome dark eyes were alive now with more than worry. One whole brilliantined line of hair stuck out from the black gloss like the ruffled crest of a cormorant.

He sat down with emphasis, and laughed at his blotting-pad.

'I mean, I ask you, when we've all got our ball-points', he tittered, 'the money I could save round this joint.'

'Steady on, Dad, said Hearst.

The women all looked up with wide-open eyes.

'No!' they all said as one. 'Has it come? Is it a boy?'

Mansford looked fiercely at Hearst:

'You see? You've made me premature. No,' he said. 'No such luck. It's pretty near, though.'

Tiny Hearst took out an Imperial Mint, popped this between his lips, and liquidly intoned:

'Our Pater Familiar has been indulging in liquid refreshment in no uncertain terms. As a Temperance man myself, I—'

'It's the strain,' muttered Mansford, glazed-eyed. 'Poor girl.'

'Then why add to your worries with these blotters?' sucked Tiny. 'We don't want any more Time and Motion round here. No more Red Hells, thank you. "Repaint your Powder Rooms eruptivewise," ' he intoned in a kind of American accent, mimicking the efficiency expert, ' "to combat lingering personalwise" . . .'

He added: 'Result? No Time for a Motion! If you will pardon my French, ladies?'

They all laughed—a little wildly. It was an old office joke: but never before had it been repeated in mixed company. A sign things were livening up.

Mansford cupped his mouth with his hand and leant over to Hearst, shaking like a jelly:

'Put a tourniquet round it,' he whispered, 'and wait till you get home.'

Miss Cook sniffed: 'Some people seem to have had one too many bull's-eyes.'

'I enjoined our friend,' chuckled Mansford, 'to a glass of peppermint. I think it's knocked his nut off.'

'Merry ante-Christmas,' drawled a new voice, 'and mind the "e".'

It was Mark Deane, their Public Relations Manager, passing through with the Chemical Director Alec Quentin to the latter's office. Mark was a lively young man with a casual manner bred of a moneyed education. Also referred to as their Public Schools Manager: and by Mavis Cook as 'the matinée idol'. As H. J.'s nephew, guilt made him despise his excellent job. He had orange hair, a winning way, and his well-cut suit was a shade darker than anyone else's in the office.

As he came in, Sandra sat up straighter. His position and good looks alone might have demanded this: but in the past Mark had also seemed to take an interest in her, he often stopped for a chat. This was a bit of a mystery. He had never made an advance.

'Any luck?' he asked Mansford as he passed.

Mansford shook his head, though still shaking with laughter about the tourniquet. Mark looked at him with interest:

'Heavens, man, you don't really think you can get out of it at this late hour, do you?' He turned to Quentin. 'Miracles,' he said, 'seasonable, but can you see Joseph grinning like that?'

Quentin's gold-rimmed glasses glittered, as if laughing. His mouth seldom had time to, he was so busy, so eager.

'Barbiturates,' he piped in a high-pitched Scottish accent, 'bonny wee barbies.'

But Hearst shook his head at them:

'The author is celebrating prematurely. *With Pipe and Pram in Darkest Penge* by R. A. P. Mansford is yet in the embryonic stage.'

Mansford growled. Sandra thought: What on earth are they saying? But she laughed. And then the two men passed on, Quentin eagerly bouncing on his toes, Mark casually taking his time—it was astonishing that they reached the door of Quentin's office at exactly the same time.

Quentin went in first, keen to get on with something. He was a freckled chestnut-coloured man, whose forward-peering face with its scrub of moustache collected knowledge with the assiduity of a squirrel collecting nuts: he wore a tawny tweed suit in the office, and this increased that effect.

Miss Cook rose to follow him, she was his personal assistant.

Jill called after her: 'Careful! He looks inspired!'

It was a reference to Quentin's compulsive urge to test out experimental products on Mavis's face, as being the most handy. He had a small laboratory in one corner of his office. Sometimes, after a supposed period of dictation, she would emerge from the office with one eye blue and the other green, slashed and bloody with different lipsticks, as if she had been fighting for her honour.

Just then H. J. and Monica came back laughing over something, rosy. Mavis paused to let them pass through to the inner offices. She pretended not to look, but her eyes sharpened. Had they just met in the lift? Or had they had lunch together? That poor man looks tired out, she thought.

Thus at Allasol on the twenty-third of December it became half-past three o'clock by the red-needling clock, and all staff present.

Work was over for another year. There was a general relaxing—already little levities had occurred and soon, as everyone knew, the party would begin, and Christmas come suddenly into being, bang.

Yet there was one thing first to wait for, the Bonus Round, the Personal Message.

And at twenty-to-four H. J. came out of his office, carrying a little tray full of envelopes, looking stern and holy, and walking backwards.

He always made a point of handing out the envelopes personally. Now that the bonus was halved, a less courageous man might have delegated the task. But H. J. believed that this was music which should be faced: also that his personal charm and presence might temper the disappointment. He came out backwards only because he was holding the tray, and wished a hand for the door knob.

Monica Naseby followed with a second tray, smiling bravely, determined to allay the desperate moment with good cheer.

83

Sandra's heart leapt into her mouth as she saw them. She swallowed it, and looked guiltily at Jill. Had Jill told?

Then H. J. winked at her. She coloured with pride. For a moment she forgot her immediate troubles, and her chin, small and pointed, raised itself a shade higher. She was there, behind him.

V

H. J. had breezed out of the inner office at a kind of trot. He stopped sharp outside the invisible cubicles of his Sales Manager and his London and Southern Area Sales Manager. Then he crossed at a more formal pace the threshold marked out by the carpet-layer, and could now be seen bent over their desks handing them their packets and speaking in an urgent whisper.

As he received his Message, Hearst's eyes half closed and his whole big face smiled inwardly, as if he had eaten a steak and kidney pudding with only one piece of kidney in it, and knew this.

Ralph Mansford turned a paler shade of grey within his anguish and good looks, as he smiled his thanks.

And when H. J. turned again and made for Mavis Cook, his own face was also racked with distress, jowls drawn down in pain, big steel-grey eyes blind with resolution. He had sold himself with his own story.

Now he was mumbling to Mavis Cook:

'. . . not what we had hoped . . . pull together . . . consolidation . . . expansion. . . .'

Behind him, Monica's cheerful resilience destroyed this careful atmosphere of mutual distress by laughing back to the shaken Mansford:

'Not to worry, Papa. You'll be stinking with family allowances before the year's out—many a father gives up work altogether!'

Mansford made a brave attempt:

'Call that giving up work?

Sandra, over-alert, relieved now that the secret was out, noted a new flash of concern in Mavis's glasses.

'Yes, it's him she's wedded to, not the office,' she told herself. 'Oh, poor dear Mavis.'

Jill received her bonus with a brave fresh smile.

'Thanks *ever* so much, Mr Deane,' she trilled. And added, 'Needs must when the devil drives.'

H. J. gave her a sharp look and moved on towards the outer passage. Monica followed, but saying in the hearing of all:

'I shouldn't really do the whole round if I were you Mr Deane.'

'But I *want* to!' H. J. replied, a twinkle showing beneath his crucified eyebrows. Then he added: 'Why not?'

He was not one for avoiding responsibilities. But so far it had not been so pleasant as in previous years. He missed this affirmative pleasure, the glow of generosity, the warmth of gratitude.

Monica resolutely helped him:

'Well, you've got one or two things to finish up— that Ruby Nearness lipstick survey. We need you here for the Party, you know.'

That word 'need'! Excellent little woman! H. J. put on his doubtful look—lower-lip above upper, considerative.

'W-e-ell, if you say so,' he said. 'I'll go as far as Mailing, and you can do downstairs. And the Pool too, of course,' he added casually.

At this word, Monica's hazel eyes changed colour. Selflessly planning H. J.'s escape, she had forgotten the hazards of the Pool. Now she straightened her straight back, and, compact and soignée on her short legs, led the way. H. J. lumbered athletically after her, big and easy, grim and serious.

For he also carried with him all the hidden troubles of an executive. The manifold manipulations of the expanding Mission, and many a seasonable trouble. Not for him the simplicity of a Christmas holiday. There was the problem of investments, with a lagging market simply because the posts were late at the Stock Exchange. Or not? And down-tools at the new factory—what if the weather got angry with new the cement? And so on and on, never stopping, never like a nice neat nine to five job and no worries after five. And on top of it all, landed with a lot of damned leather, stuff that wouldn't wear out. Crust Skivers. And the Warble Fly.

Left with their packets, his loyal staff reacted in various ways.

Mavis Cook put her packet neatly in her bag, knowing that she must now forego a theatre outing with her friends the Cranberries. However, she was so used to compromise and sacrifice that quite mildly she saw how it would make a nice quiet evening at home instead. Much more important was that poor man's health.

Jill Jenkins made a down-mouthed pout and said her final goodbyes to a twin-set she had her eye on. But she was not really worried. Mums and Daddy would fork out some kind of compensation. Besides, it was Christmas, wasn't it? Nothing was going to get *her* down. Soonest said least mended, she told herself.

Nor was Tiny Hearst hard hit. As a widower the money would only go to his savings to be spent at a time he foresaw but could not visualise, when he should be seventy. What he did feel with sudden passion was something described in his mind as 'wheels within wheels', and which now occasioned an odd scornful noise, a kind of hrroumph.

But Ralph Mansford was horrified. He wanted every penny at the moment. Now, at one stroke, he was suddenly many pounds short. He wanted to cry. But, like everything else, like the poor pain of his girl and the anxieties of uncharted fatherhood ahead, he could do nothing. He was anaesthetised by frustration. He simply sat there swearing under his breath, in rhythm, without emphasis, and reading over and over again the Christmas message of goodwill typed on his packet.

Sandra herself was flummoxed. Although she had known about it earlier, the actual sight of the packet disturbed her. She had earmarked the missing money for a new frock. Yet here she was wearing a new frock. Which cancelled out. She felt robbed of profit and compensated for loss. Trying to work this out, she had perhaps as bad a time of it as anyone.

Sighs then, and a short silence as there came into play the national aptitude for shouldering trouble with a grin and a grumble—cloaking an instinct to seek immediately, with no wasted emotion, the most comfortable alternative. Everybody, like Mavis Cook and her 'quiet evening', concentrated on small mercies. And two among the five reached down beneath their desk to draw forth bottles, Tiny Hearst and Mavis Cook, oddly the Temperance man and the tea-addict. But perhaps their unaccustomed bottles worried them, or perhaps they had a clearer view of alcohol as medicine. Whatever the reason, the first two corks were drawn at Allasol that afternoon at four o'clock precisely.

'Allow me to proffer you a modicum,' chanted Hearst pouring Portuguese claret into a cardboard cup and handing this to Mansford, 'of what the doctor ordered.'

Mavis Cook passed to Jill Jenkins ginger wine in a glass borrowed from the Red Hell, muttering between pursed lips the words: 'Bottoms up.'

Jill brought out a big champagne-like bottle of sparkling cider, and Sandra a rich South African sherry. Mansford produced from a straw turkey bag three dark and sturdy quarts of brown ale.

Mavis Cook placed out on her desk an open box of green peppermint jellies, and Tiny Hearst undid dates and a wooden box of candied peel. Mavis had also brought some potted shrimps.

Then Sandra went into Monica's office where a dozen new glasses lay in sawdust and straw, and everyone poured everyone else a drink and cheerohed each other and drank, spitting out little bits of cork and wood.

'Well,' Mansford suddenly muttered, as brown ale and sherry fired inside him, 'I don't see how you can expand and consolidate at the same time.'

'Think of your missus,' Hearst said.

'You consolidate,' Mavis sniffed, '*to* expand. Or you expand *to* consolidate—with credit facilities. Surely the great financial brain opposite is aware of this.'

'All I'm aware of,' Tiny said, popping his eyes right out round from under the long pale lashes, 'is wheels within wheels. With special reference to a certain motorcar by Bentley the personal property of an individual to wit Mister Honest Jack. I don't see *that* machine suddenly bereft of half its wheels.'

Sandra said: 'Well, you're not going home on half a bus are you? Just because you've got half a packet?'

'Half a bus is better than no—' Mavis began with a laugh, then scrambled to her feet, for the orange curls of Mark Deane had come round the partition corner and he was frowning—Mavis quickly put a glass of ginger wine in his hand, hoping to divert him from what Hearst had said.

But Mark was frowning for a very different reason, which he had to keep to himself. The bonus was halved, but the directors had voted themselves at a recent board meeting an increase of fees. A 'normal' increase, of course. Resentment against his nepotic situation and a sense of a humane justice riled in him. But now the frown remained for yet another reason, the ginger wine. He had just come from his own section, where politeness had forced him to accept offerings of Spanish Chablis and Australian Burgundy. Where would it end? All we need is a Norwegian Chianti, he told himself.

'Thank you, Mave,' he said. 'Here's to the better half, Ralph.'

Their eyes dropped to the half-bonus packet. Mark shook his head:

'Not *that* one. Wouldn't say no to twins there.'

'Don't say that word, don't say it, Mark. You'll have a brown with me?'

He poured it. Mark thought, 'Christ' and said 'God, bless.'

'Candied peel?' Hearst shouted to him, relieved that his remark about Uncle's Bentley seemed to be passed over.

Mark showed his glass-filled hands.

'I haven't got two pairs of ulcers,' he pleaded.

Just then H. J. came back, and again backwards.

Bottom first, bent listening to where he had come from, stepping quiet on raised toes, head cocked anxious as a big bull bird. Suddenly he jerked to a stop as a new sound, what he must have been listening for, came rising softly at first then echoing up loud like a thunderous roll of distant breaking waves, voices in unison singing *Nearer My God to Thee*.

H. J. let out a great guttural sigh, like a man all in, turned, saw he was seen—he had not realised he had backed so far—and gave a hollow laugh.

'The Pool,' he said.

'Drink?' said Mavis, already there.

'Need it,' he said, and tossed back the glass. Purple blood flooded across his face. It was the ginger wine. An invisible force seemed to strike the back of his head, jolting it forward. He looked quickly at the glass, and at Miss Cook.

'Thanks,' he said, 'thanks.'

Nearer My God to Thee came and went with the regularity of a stormy sea.

'That damned *Lusitania* film,' Monica swore as she came in, slinging her empty tray down on a filing cabinet. She looked haggard. 'They opened their packets and all started up at once. How do those kids know the *words* of everything?'

'Discs,' said Jill.

'Lennie Bridesmeat did *Nearer My God* on Stereophone,' Sandra said, 'vocal and electric.'

'Electric?'

'Guitar. That shanty's got all the good kids going.'

'Shanty?' burst Mark. 'I suppose Bridesmeat's got a choir hauling the mainsheet *behind* the paddling Marines.'

'The what?'

'Well, didn't the Marines go down to attention playing the hymn? Wasn't that the story?'

Monica Naseby patted her ruffled hair straight.

'You've no call to go laughing at *that*,' she said. 'Nobody has. And especially you, bright boy, with your Lordosis Slips. That's what started it, the lord in your lovely Praise the Lordosis.'

The hymn was swelling below, now filling the resonant office passages like a cathedral choir. 'It makes your blood run cold,' she said.

'Lordosis?' shot Tiny, hiccupping through a mouthful of candied peel.

'The Lordosis Slips,' Mark said, 'were for anti-lordosis insurance, cushions and whatnot.'

'Insurance,' H. J. put in loudly, nodding.

Monica saw she had made a mistake in talking of these slips. No one but H. J. and Mark knew that at a Board Meeting on the bonus reduction it had been agreed that something extra had to be done for the Pool, for these young typists were difficult to keep, they had no such loyalties as the more skilled staff, and would 'down tools as soon as panties'—in Mark's after-lunch phrase—and be off at the smell of a half-bonus.

So Mark had put up the idea that they ran the special risk of lordosis, occupational disease of typists, a stiffening of the spine leading later to an outward projection of the bottom. He had suggested an extra payment to cover cushion-buying and insurance against this. It would be left to them to spend the money—which of course they would pocket. If anyone questioned the word lordosis, a little wink would put this right. It was agreed that no one would take it too seriously. It was only remarkable that Mark and H. J. approached the idea so gravely themselves. Accustomed to modern methods of staff-retention—luncheon vouchers, holiday vouchers, superannuation and health schemes, Top-Hat—such official bribery scarcely seemed to them out of the way. Nor did the dredging up of a little-known disease—their own advertising had trained them well.

'And do you know,' Monica laughed up across the awkwardness, 'that sign on the wall saying THINK? One of those kids crossed the TH out and put an S.'

Nearer My God to Thee swelled louder, nearer, receded, as everybody laughed, too loud and uneasily, at this

binding of the dooms of Allasol and the *Lusitania*.
'Man the lifeboats!' H. J. called.

'And splice the mainbrace,' boomed Mavis and there
was a renewed clinking and gurgling as glasses and cups
were refilled. They began to leave their chairs to perch on
corners of desks, or on the lowest filing cabinets, and
H. J. sent Monica in for a half dozen claret he had ready,
for he had thought this to be the best available solvent
for the diversity about—a Cherry Heering and a British
Port from the Mailing Department already lay beneath
his surgical belt.

It began to look for the first time as if a party was in
progress. The lights were switched on, and turned the
darkening room abrupt yellow. Festive tissues and
coloured wrappings lay everywhere. Bottles and sweets
and bits of food winked among typewriters and folders
and files. There was a fuzz of smoke. Tin-lid ash-trays
were already full, ash was getting among the paper-clips.

Yet they were still in everyday office clothes—and this
struck a note both abandoned and dreary at the same time.

There would soon be a coming and going between
departments, people drifting here and there with bottles
in their hands. Shop talk fell away, Christmas was in
the air, and snatches of talk came to Sandra, through
the growing buzz, as she wondered whom to speak
with.

'Well, we've painted and polished a hundred thousand
mixed housewives and daughters for another year—'
'And made them smell the sweeter—'

'So perhaps we can sit back for an hour or two. They'll understand, I hope.'

'Oh, they're *so* understanding.'

'I couldn't fail to disagree with you less.'

'I tell you it's true, they said so on the telly.'

'Oh—in that case.'

'We'll take it easily, now the cards are done and the presents are done and the decorations done and the food done. Pull down the blinds.'

'You off anywhere for Christmas?'

'No. My wife's brother's coming, with their four girls.'

'Oh, *that*'ll be fun.'

'Until the S.P.C.C. puts its nose in.'

'Chin chin.'

'Mud in it.'

Mavis had begun to go on about an Indian veil she had bought for her sister-in-law-down-at-Portsmouth. Sandra found her eyes on the clock, on that red needle hurrying round, slow in its fast way, and suddenly she remembered, Bun's coming *here*, oh Lord. Apart from anything else, it was going to be embarrassing to have him run the gauntlet of the office eye. It was not like introducing Bun to ordinary friends. He would be like a museum exhibit. Suddenly she realised that Bun was part of her 'mantelpiece'—and laughed again at herself, at that crazy idea.

Should she go down and tell the red-eyed old commissionaire to let her know when Bun arrived, instead of sending Bun up? Or even—tell him to tell Bun she had left! She felt again how things were pressing in on her. First Nevile and that parcel, now Bun coming. Forcing her. I won't see him, she suddenly swore.

'Mlle Sandra? A drop of official brew? A quite unassuming claret, I understand,' Monica's face was saying close to hers. She could see that thick tongue rolled inside the rouge of her pouting lower lip. H. J.'s claret bottle clinked at her glass. Then Monica's smart voice droning liquidly:

'Why, Marge, *what* a pretty brooch!'

Bitch: she'd said it only so as not to notice the new dress, it was an old brooch.

'Why, Monnie, how nice of you. But it's a lot older than this here wine, I should say. Or shouldn't I?' she giggled.

Monica's eyes flashed but she pealed with laughter. Hearst brandished his bonus-packet:

'Beggars can't be . . .'

Then someone put the lights out. Startled cries in the sudden new dusk. And Mark Deane took her arm and led her towards the window.

Mark Deane! Mark's fingers on her elbow, and all her nerves electric.

'I put the lights out,' Mark said, 'because—look at that! What do you think of *that*, Sandra?'

Outside, where the tiled well-wall finished, the last dying light had clouded sky and city with an embery cold fire that suggested snow and blue wood-smoke. The shapes of distant buildings lost their hardness, they might have been cut from purple felt: here and there red chimneys blazed out, but mostly it was purple-grey slate, grey stone, brown brick. Cold—but picturesque, and she thought instantly of fuzzily-printed Christmas scenes on cards.

'Oh, lovely,' she breathed, meaning it, for this picture framed in the window brought back memories of the books read in childhood, and of the excitement of Christmas shopping. Cold nose, red shops, wool gloves wet with snow. But Mark was whispering:

'Birkett-Foster comes to town.'

'Mm,' she said, not knowing what this could mean. The dream receded, nervous nearness returned. She could feel the colour of his hair. He had a nice voice, a bit snooty. But you never knew what he was thinking. Sometimes she had wondered whether he was laughing at her all the time. There had been odd moments in the past, like the time he had told her about that film, giggling away about a nurse-doctor romance where the hero-doctor in a green mask had made eyes at his nurse, while performing a stomach operation. He had been removing entrails with bloody instruments—and the audience all sucking away at sweets and lollies as hard as they could.

'But why not?' Sandra had said.

'What—red giblets and ice-lollies? Don't you see?'

Sandra had said what she thought:

'But they *liked* the film, and they *like* their lollies. And it's good business for the cinema. I don't see what's so funny.'

He had sighed.

'Oh, Sandra,' he said. 'Oh, poker face.'

Now what had that meant? Had he not taken her seriously, or had he seriously been taken in?

Now he was going on again:

'He pictured winter so well. A real romantic. No, a romantic realist.'

She was about to risk: 'He could certainly use a camera,' but stopped herself as Mark went on:

'An engraver has a good chance with snow. A matching coldness—we even use the word "engraved" to describe a winter's scene.'

He sighed:

'Still, I don't suppose you'll be seeing much snow this year. I will though—tomorrow'll see me through the great Swiss watch-belt to the Engadine.'

'Oh?' said Sandra sharply. Did he think he was the only one who could go off abroad? 'I may be off too,' she said.

'Really?' he asked, not masking too well his surprise.

'Sarawak,' she nonchalantly said, and bit her tongue. Great heavens—to H. J.'s nephew! Had she let the cat out of the bag? Had she given herself the sack?

'Droves of snow that-a-way, I imagine,' he smiled down at her.

She pouted. 'But I don't think I'll go.'

'Just like that?'

'Just like what?'

His hair was quietly flaming against the grey window, as a flower burns cool in the moonlight. He moved it down towards her and laughed:

'You are a one, Sand-in-my-eyes. I thought you meant it for a moment.'

She could see his teeth very close in the half-dark.

'Did you?' she said. And her heart fluttered as what was happening appeared to her in capital letters: Here and Now Mark Deane the Public Relations Manager and Heir to Allasol was leaning over her with a kind of lewd sneer.

'Sandra,' he murmured, 'I don't think I'll ever get to the bottom of you.'

'A reserved seat, kind sir,' she bubbled.

Heavens! What was talking—the wine? Mark chuckled. And then suddenly all the lights came on again.

'Vandals!' he muttered. She saw the lewd sneer was no more than a smile. He sighed: 'Let's have another drink.'

She moved away from the window with regret: but this was caused as much by something she had just noticed through the window, as by Mark.

Down deep below in the dusky well she had spotted one bright-lit window where another party was being held. Sudden brightness indeed! The other windows paled before this bright rich yellow blaze of light, and she could see what seemed most glamorous smart women chatting to and fro in cocktail dresses, while elegant black-coated men like floor walkers carried bottles about. There seemed to be music, silenced by glass: gestures suggested a shaking and singing—altogether the windows gave the effect of a big coloured television screen with the sound switched off.

It was the kind of party Sandra's imagination longed

for. How so exotic there? Possibly a wholesale dress house? Now when she turned round, the room at Allasol looked drab indeed. Bottles, Christmas paper, laughter— but these were all people she knew, and still dressed in office clothes she knew so well, and each with an office personality, or that half-personality you could never properly get hold of. It was going to be a dull show. Nothing, nothing would happen.

'Look at that chart above Ralph's head!' Mark said. 'The sharp red downward dip—like a Damoclean sword.'

'Ha ha,' she laughed, 'oh ha ha.'

Sandra! Throw back your head with its lustrous coiffure, let fly from your painted face! Let fly what? she thought hopelessly.

'Sales charts, sales charts—can't we do better than that?' Mark said, looking for a bottle. 'Now the advertising agency we use, which it is my sick pleasure to visit every week of my life, manages a much brighter effect. Illingworth's plastered the wall with still lifes.'

'Really?' she said, gritting her teeth.

'A fine representative collection. Apples and oranges and bottles, bottles and oranges and apples, oranges and apples and bottles wherever you look. It looks like the lair of a drunken greengrocer. Drop of red ink?'

'Thanks,' she said, and tossed back the glass.

'I say,' Mark said.

You'll say, will you? she thought. What'll you say? What'll you say a girl wants to hear, I don't think. My God, I'll say something in a moment, she swore. It's now or never. Inside, she began to rage. Her whole eventless life seemed suddenly narrowed down to this party. She gave a great two-handed tug at the girdle inside her dress, reached for the nearest bottle, British Port, gushed herself a glassful and tossed it down. But *careful*, she said to herself even then, remember the Night You Passed Out. . . .

Then Mavis Cook was hissing in her ear:

'I heard her, I heard Monnie say that about your brooch. The bitch!'

'Why, *Mavis*!' she said, shocked. A strange fire of venom glittered behind Mavis's glasses.

'I'll Mavis you,' she said, patches of red angrily dolling her white cheeks, grey hair a strand astray. 'If you don't give her a piece of your mind, *I* will.'

'A piece of yours, or a piece of mine?' Sandra giggled.

'That poor man!' Miss Cook said, breathing hard.

And then there was Jill Jenkins, her rose face flushed with wine, pouring claret into Mavis's glass.

'A little of what you fancy that does you good?' she laughed.

Then the laugh broke into a wide placid yawn.

'Well,' she sighed, with an up and down soughing sound, placid as a suburban afternoon, 'well, it's quite a do, isn't it?'

H. J.'s all right,' said Sandra in mischief to Mavis Cook, 'don't you worry about H. J.'

'*Not* worry about Mr Deane? Who's our life and breath, our bread and butter?' Mavis cried. 'Where's that Monica?'

'Steady on!' Mark put in. 'Why here's your Alec Quentin needs you more by the look of it.'

Quentin had just come out of his office, and was squirreling eagerly round with a glass of wine and a packet of white powder, which he held demonstrating a little experiment.

'Simple', he was saying, his inquisitive eyes peering down at the glass. 'You take a simple glass of claret, nothing up your sleeves, add a heaped saltspoonful of bicarbonate of soda—and hey presto! Sparkling Vouvray!'

As he spoke he dropped the white powder into the red wine and this immediately fizzed, turning a richer-looking purple, with a champagne-like foam.

'Like this,' he added, 'any old Hock makes an impassable champagne.'

There was clapping. Mavis joined in, momentarily mollified, and accepted the glass. Quentin was popular. Interested in everything but individual persons, he bustled through life without making much personal contact. He never made people nervous; he was innocent by default, always away with some idea. A squirrel, someone had once said, off his nut.

'Hup!' Mavis said. 'Windigestion'.

'There!' Quentin said, 'Just like the real thing!'

'Hello, Ralph's looking rather red in the face! Nearness 3 Cannibale, if I don't deceive myself.'

Ralph Mansford had burst in, wiping lipstick off his cheek.

'My God, the switchboard's murder!' he gasped, 'I went down to make sure they were putting calls up here and the two of them fell on me like wolves. Elaine Dawkin's got a bunch of mistletoe tied right on to that little black trumpet thing strapped to her bosom, so help me.'

'Any news yet?' Sandra asked.

'Nix,' he said. 'But how about you? That fellow who was having a baby all morning?'

Sandra flinched.

'A miscarriage, at about noon,' she said.

She regretted it. Ralph looked away.

Jill hissed in her ear: 'Of justice?'

'Jill!' she gasped.

And Mark Deane suddenly sang, simply because he wanted something to sing:

'Sandra's off to Sarawak for the solstice.'

She froze.

Jill's eyes popped wide open with glee. But Monica Naseby had come up and hers narrowed.

'Sarawak?' she said.

Sandra said too quickly: 'I never said any such thing—'

'Just for the solstice?' Monica smiled.

Sandra did not like the sound of that word in any case. But before she could speak, Monica went on:

'Isn't Sarawak where your fiancé might be bound for, didn't you tell me once? You wouldn't be gliding out on us, would you?'

Sandra laughed: 'What—give up a peach of a job like this to go riding elephants? I wasn't born yest—'

Jill was shaking her head: 'No elephants,' she hissed.

'What d'you mean, no elephants,' Sandra said hotly.

'No elephants in Sarawak,' Jill said, 'A man told me.'

'Phew—how far can you go?' whistled Mark. 'But what kind of a place can it be, no elephants?'

When fortunately the mailing clerk Bossom came dancing in with his friend, Bone, to complete a short step routine by the door.

'A glass of po-oit?' these two ended, in close harmony.

Everyone turned in wonder.

Messrs Bone and Bossom stood poised as if carrying straw hat and cane. Jollily tipsy, they were at the stage that likes to pretend it is drunk.

H. J. on the far side of the room clapped his jovial hands, and nodded to Monica to give them a couple of glasses. Bone crumpled with shyness. Even Bossom flinched, but then regained himself and took his glass with a fine theatrical bow. They were a well-known double-act in the office. Bone was like a fleshy shadow attached to the virile Bossom, and it was Bone who was so hopelessly in love with Sandra. She now went straight to him, panicking from Monica, and slipped her arm in his. He seemed to glisten brighter with youthful oils, and he turned a shade paler. This had never, never happened before. Tiny Hearst laboriously helped them out with:

'Entrez, Mr Outray. And the outrageous Mr Intray!'

'Happy as bank-larks,' Mark tried.

For a moment the solstice was forgotten. Sandra herself had drunk much more than usual, and on top of a good lunch. Monica might be dangerous—but for the moment she chose to forget that too. Much more important was Bun's imminent arrival: and a certain change that had come over the party.

It was definitely easing. Glasses were balancing on

round ink-erasers, bottles were leaving rings on buff manila files—and people were showing the edges of their mantelpieces. Mavis Cook had come into the clear battling for H. J., and H. J. himself had relaxed from twinkling to become like any other big tired man, heavy-jowled, like a weary boxer-dog. And Monica was fussing him like an equal—confirming many a suspicion.

Then Sandra saw that Jill had slung a rope of pearls beneath her flushed face, and now gazed at Mark Deane between bruised-looking eyelids! Ralph Mansford was looking more worried than ever, and drinking like a real father-to-be. And here was Tiny Hearst edging his huge bulk up against H. J., standing with hands in pockets and telling him exactly what he, personally, Hearst himself thought about the commissionaire Bletch below taking half an hour off for tea just when the lift was needed most.

H. J. repeated every so often: 'Of course, of course. Still the chap's got to have his tea sometime, eh?' While he thought: 'They're making plastic leather as good as the real stuff nowadays—better, in fact, it *breaks*. My bloody real stuff lasts.'

Mansford opened his handsome mouth in the hard high cackle of a man losing his wits:

'He could always have high tea on the sixth,' he screamed.

If things were moving like this, Sandra suddenly thought she must protect, yes protect Bun from so many new people. He would just *hate* it, she thought, as she saw that she might finally enjoy herself. Magical compassion! Bone's eyes burned at her under fat lids—she drew her arm away, tossed her head and hurried out past the hyacinths to where the lift had its 'Not Working' sign up.

Commissionaire Bletch must have been taking a seasonable Christmas rest. But he was usually to be found in his hole near the front door, brewing tea or reading his racing. So she clattered her way down the empty stone-echoing stairway towards the ground floor, round and round the iron lift-shaft, between the Victorianly chocolate-and-cream-painted walls to the hall panelled with mahogany and with a rich mosaic floor.

On the way she could still hear the Pool, far above—a confused chitter, like a vast aviary, together with a steady thud as they jived. *Nearer My God* was long over: now somebody's transistor made the pace.

The sign 'Not Working' had disturbed Bletch—for who was not working?—and so he had stencilled an enormous placard OUT OF ORDER for the main lift door. Now his dark blue back was bent over a little gas-ring in his cubby-hole full of light switches, paper notices, scrim and tea-cups.

'Excuse me, sarge!' Sandra called to him.

He whipped round and stared at her with eyes lidded rheumy red while one hand instinctively cupped itself to hide the cigarette he smoked.

'I'm making my tea,' he announced, as if that closed whatever matter had not yet been opened.

'Don't worry about me, sergeant,' Sandra said smiling her best and freshest, 'but I just wanted to ask a favour.'

His whole face stiffened. It was as if 'The Queen' was about to be played. He knew all about favours.

'Yes, sergeant. You see if a young man called Bun—I mean, Stanbetter, comes asking for Allasol or me, would you please tell him I've left?'

'What—left Allasol?'

'Me? Left Allasol?' she said startled. 'No—I mean, say I've gone for the afternoon.'

'Now, miss, I haven't got all day. When's he expected?'

'Now! And he's tall and he's got a sort of—' she found suddenly she could not at all describe Bun—'he's clean-shaven, name of Stanbetter, and he'll be coming soon. He's got a piece of hair hanging down on his forehead. Just tell him I've gone.'

She closed one set of mascaraed lids in a conspiratorial wink. It looked as if she had been given a sudden black eye. The commissionaire looked at her coldly.

'Piece of hair on his forehead, eh? *If* I should see this gentleman, *when* he should appear, I'll do my best, miss.'

And then suddenly one rheumy red eye flickered a wink back at her.

'Thanks awfully,' Sandra smiled, and turned with a busy swirl back to the stairs.

His red old eyes followed her. A slight pursing of lips beneath the sore-looking scrub of moustache showed he was smiling. '*If* I should see this gentleman *when*,' he said to himself. 'That's in future, ain't it?'

Five minutes previously he had testily demonstrated to a gentleman with a lock of hair on his brow the general direction of Allasol, though on malicious purpose the wrong one, a floor and a passage out.

Now he watched with satisfaction Sandra's legs disappearing up the stairs again.

'Get in, Nob, it's your birthday,' he growled, and turned back into his hole where from beneath the Racing Chronicle he drew into the open a bottle of rum, and took a well-deserved swig. Then he shook his head at the bottle. He had prostate trouble, he would suffer for it later on.

VI

SANDRA returned to Allasol feeling she had done the right thing. She would phone Bun at home later. It would not be fair, no, not fair to leave him dangling his toes so near Christmas. Nor sensible.

And Nevile Wrasse?

As she re-entered the office a warm spirituous essence greeted her, rich after the iron and stone of the corridor outside. No more the papery india-rubber smell—it smelled of lights and drinks and smoke, like a real party.

Everybody was talking at once. Half-known faces had drifted in from other departments. There was a feeling, almost exciting, of strangers. Somebody had brought a bucket of water to rinse the glasses, and this gave a cheerful tinny bing and swosh from time to time.

'You use peas?' a Production man was saying to Quentin.

'No, grains. Easier to hod-in.'

'They come smaller,' the other said. 'Get much clinker?'

A coy look came across Quentin's face:

'You know,' he confessed with bright eyes, 'I *like* my clinker. When it comes out all in one piece, glowing red-hot. . . .'

'How often d'you riddle?'

Sandra passed on.

'Hey,' yelled Jill with a bottle, 'a little of what you fancy?' She held out a glass and poured from a brown bottle with a green label. More ginger wine, Sandra thought, and tossed it straight back. But it was Irish whiskey.

While she was coughing, she heard Tiny Hearst say to Mansford:

'Look, old man, I'm not telling a lie. No W in the Spanish alphabet. And here you have our Potteries exporting the water-closet for the first time beyond the Pyrenees. This is a revolutionary moment. The Spaniards are a proud people. And they are proud of this modern acquisition—they won't have them called anything else but W.C. Still call them *El Vater* today. Remember—no W in the Spanish alphabet. So there's this old fellow told me he went visiting down there, he was rep. for a Staffordshire sanitary engineer, and took a big bag of brass Ws with him. Sold them on the side, see, made a little fortune over the years—Navarre, Aragon, Old and New and for all I know W. Castile. Bit of a job matching up with the Spanish Cs, he used to say.'

Mansford shook his head.

'No good,' he said.

'I should jolly well think not,' Sandra said to herself. 'First their boilers, now this. Call it a party.'

'Not taken your mind off it? Not a bit?' Hearst asked Mansford.

He shook his head. Hearst took a deep breath, and clenched his teeth on a large lump of nougat.

'We can,' he said, 'but persist. Did I ever tell you of the drive-in brothel in Barcelona? No kidding. Drive your car in, through bead curtains and all. First mothel in the world.'

Sandra laughed. At least the word brothel was a cue for laughter. And the whiskey had warmed her.

'Keep the party clean,' she giggled.

'As the undertaker said to the laying-out lady,' Hearst murmured.

'The party of the last part?' she laughed quick back. And managed a wink at Mark, a smile for Monica and H. J., and a cold eye at Bone almost at the same time. She suddenly felt fine.

'Yoops!' she said all round. 'How goes the yackety-yack?'

Five faces melon-mouthed with smiles round her. Even H. J. spread his beefy muscle of a face in a wide grin. 'Replaceable durables' he was thinking, this formula having occurred to him as a kind of magic.

She abruptly blossomed.

Bossom was singing a line of Gilbert and Sullivan just behind her—she joined in reckless. And the line came out:

'A policeman shot is not a happy one.'

This bent everyone in two.

'Oh—oh, *very* true.'

'Sandra, *please!*'

'Sandra!' and Bone's eyes bulged wide open with admiration.

H. J. jovially said: 'Mark that one up!'

'So much light, and under such a bushel,' Mark cooed shamelessly.

'A bushel,' Monica purred over her big tongue, 'of three coats Allasol's best Pancake.'

'You're forgetting the Mission's Muscovy Mascara,' Sandra laughed sweetly. 'Oh, Mavis, how exotic!'

For Miss Cook had edged in showing the gilded corner of an Indian veil protruding from an envelope. 'It's for my sister-in-law,' said Mavis, 'down at Portsmouth.'

Cries of delight, and Mavis was tempted to pull the veil a shade more from the envelope.

'Careful,' said Monica, 'You'll never fold it again.'

'Hung for a sheep, says I,' Mavis growled, and pulled it out wide open like a flag, shimmering gold and pink and orange, dazzling and drawing all eyes. She turned to Sandra, hiccupped and said:

'Try it, Marge, I want to see!'

The veil went round and like a halo all over her hair. She lowered her green lids to look mysterious as Indian ladies she had seen in chilly saris.

She stood posed quite still for brilliant seconds, and she looked truly beautiful. Mouths ooed and nummed noises of appreciation, while her mind managed to make herself for Mark and H. J. a great professional beauty, for Bone a distant queen, for Monica an ace-trumper—and at the same time for Mavis, in gratitude, a wish not to appear too glamorous.

'Lovely, lovely,' she said at last, looking only at Mavis. 'How sweet of you to let me try it—'

But suddenly Bossom, lacking limelight too long, reached out his hand and pulled the veil down right across her face, at the same time improvising Persian market music in the back of his throat.

'Who'll buy? Who'll buy? he cried, in the lively tones

of a slave-dealer. 'Eight stone lovely six! Thirty-four-twenty-one-thirty! Four-four-O!' he yelled, bestowing upon her the wheelbase of his favourite locomotive.

There was sudden quiet.

Muffled in the veil, she could see little. The room was muzzed yellow, her breath came hot and stuffy as in a Christmas game of Blind Man's Buff—voices from across the room cut extra loudly:

'A hodful of peas . . . call it a podful?' And a distracted burst from Mansford after all that time: 'A mothel! I *see*.'

Then a new voice, cheerful, called louder still:

'Two bob—I'll bid two!'

She whipped off the veil.

There in the doorway stood Bun. Bun had said it!

And with Bun stood Sue Blair, silver-haired dream girl with pink of flesh flushed pale against low-cut silver dress, holding Bun's arm.

She pointed at Sandra:

'There's your quarry, mister!' she said, smiling up at him.

'I say, thanks awfully. Hello, Sand!'

'Why, hello Bun!'

Sue walked him forward to her:

'He came wandering into the Pool—'

'A Bath Bun,' hissed Bossom.

'—so all a girl could do was rescue him,' Sue laughed.

Sandra tried to smile. It was terrible, with everyone watching. And her bubble moment broken.

'Thanks, Sue,' she tried. 'Was he heavy?'

Bun winked pleasantly down at Sue:

'I thought Miss Blair was going to throw me over her shoulder when we were jiving downstairs.'

'Jiving?' Sandra gasped, pouring sherry for them.

She gave a sweetly controlled laugh. 'Jiving?' she said, handing them each a tumblerful.

'The old one-two-three,' Sue said.

'I could have danced all night,' smiled Bun. 'It was like a fairy tale, princesses rescuing knights. Cheeroh!'

Bun's smile was even and toothy, and almost always there. His small blue eyes set back among smooth bones shone with good cheer. He raised his glass to his lips, swigged and stopped:

'Lord, I forgot! Doctor's orders.'

'Doctor's orders?' Sandra said, fearful for him.

'Just another export inject,' Bun laughed. 'Tropical Bughouse. The afternoon was free,' he added, with a special glance at Sandra.

'Really?' H. J. asked, because he had to say something, standing about there empty-handed. 'Where are you off to?'

'Ha ha ha—*ha*,' laughed Sandra over any possible answer. 'What are you *on* to's more the question! What am I to do with you bursting into a private office like this? Still, better show you round now you're here!' And she caught his hand and dragged him away off into the corridor.

'Love's young dream,' cooed Bossom after her. 'Summer nights and some are nasty.'

As she left, Sandra saw Mark and H. J. close in round Sue Blair. And both Hearst and Mansford standing peering, like outer spectators at a football match, at this dressed-up young woman they had so recently seen, in full colour, undressed.

'Oh, my dearest, I did really *have* to see you,' he said in the corridor.

'You certainly chose a fine time,' she said coldly. 'No, take your hands off me. Come on.'

Over the succulent client-catching carpets she led him, past the hyacinths, and on to a bare and draughty dead-end with a door marked FIRE.

'You're the emergency,' she snapped, 'and this is the exit.'

It was dark and chilly out on the little iron platform. Bun looked down at her thin dress and said:

'But why? Aren't you cold? Isn't that a new dress? It's pretty. Where did you—?'

'Oh, I got it—with our bonus money,' she lied, and felt instantly the angrier for it. He comes bursting in, she muttered, spoiling my fun, and just when things were hotting up. *And* he brings that blasted girl with him. And now he third-degrees me.

'Are you sure you're feeling all right?' she asked drily. 'What a time of year to get it done.'

Her face was turned away. He had to bend round to look her in the eyes: 'Sand, my love, I'm dead serious about this. It's the Big Chance. It's what I've been working for all these past years. And now I *must* take it. Don't you see a man *must.* . . .'

'Yes, I do see,' she said, but the question was labelled vaguely 'business'. Business would always rectify itself.

The high dark shapes of office buildings stood immense and desolate round them. A few uncurtained lights looked lonely as the ending of all winter days. Space echoed cold as iron beneath them.

'It's our life, Sandy,' he said quietly. 'We're going to share it—and now, now, now's the moment.'

'If it's our life, it's a lifetime,' she said, 'so I don't see where's the hurry.'

'Oh God.'

'Don't get excited.'

'Of course I'll get excited. I am excited! Don't you *see*, San?'

'For heaven's sake don't call me *that*. You know, it's *my* life as well as yours.'

He drew in a big breath. Patience, brute patience, he repeated to himself.

'Now do let's be reasonable,' he began softly.

'I am being reasonable,' she said.

'But, darling, *time* matters. Look, we've lost another day—and I don't know about plane-seats.'

'If you think I'm going to let them stick me all over with needles before Christmas, then think again,' she said. 'I've said I'm coming. I've said I'll marry you and come to ycur soppy Sarawak—what more d'you want?'

'It isn't soppy,' he said quietly. 'I want you to come *now*. Sand, I'm in love with you. I love you so much.'

She wanted to cry. A big wet lump came in her throat. Oh dear big baby, she thought.

'My Bun,' she said softly.

'There,' he said, 'there.'

He took her head in his hands and kissed her brow. She lifted her face, opened her lips.

He shook his head sadly, and kissed her gently with his own lips closed. He was breathing hard. A little cloud of white mist came from his mouth.

'I can't wait forever,' he said.

His tenderness, making her into a holiness not to be touched—he so big, yet so careful, it always moved her. Whenever in the past he had gone a little too far, he had shown a profound remorse. Yet—respected, moved, she remained untouched. Shouldn't he burst with love, over-powered by her, and tear her apart?

'A woman, Bun,' she said, gently freeing herself, 'doesn't like to be pushed. And her wedding—it's her Day, isn't it? It's the biggest day in a woman's life—and I want it to be how I want it, I don't want my face rubbed in it. You can take a horse to water, Bun.'

'Horse?' asked Bun, peering his face down, smiling now, showing all his teeth in a way she always liked, for it showed his niceness: but was it a kind of humouring smile—difficult in the half-dark to see?

'Oh, do come in out of the cold,' she shivered, 'why do we have to stand here?'

And as they went back through the rattling push-bar door she went on:

'You know I don't want a big white wedding and all that, but I do want *something*, I don't want to be bundled from a registry office into a plane and then find myself in Sarawak. I don't want to be bundled, Bu—'

She stopped suddenly. And then said crossly:

'And I've got the office to consider.'

'The office?' he said, in amazement.

'Well, the people I work with. We're not machines, you know. They'll think it rude to push off without so much as a goodbye. You get to know people pretty well when you work with them eight hours a day, day in, day out—'

'Sandra!'

He took a deep breath and spoke carefully, as if in court, or as if it was a foreign language:

'Only last Tuesday, in the Spinning Wheel, in a sober atmosphere of copper pans and Dundee Slice, you yourself raised the proposition that *you did not know these people at all*. I well remember you going on about each being three people, not one. Yes, their fleshy façade at home, their limbo-like façade at the office, and somewhere in a dark corner their real selves. Who are they? you said again and again. Then you went on about their mantelpieces—'

'You need a mental piece,' she said, airily ignoring all this. 'I've got certain obligations to my employers, haven't I? It's not just hire-fire, hire-fire.'

'Hire-fire?'

He looked round at the little corner they had chosen, at a nest of Victorian pipes painted a smart matt grey, at a red bucket of sand covered with cigarette stubs.

'I mean, there's loyalties,' she said. 'I've got to give a notice period. It wouldn't be fair not.'

She looked at him angrily. She loved him. She loved how he looked and how nice he was. She loved his forelock and his big smooth neck. She wanted to baby him—'proud-of-himself, proud-of-what?' He was the first person. Yet the last to whom she could say what simply she wanted to say: 'I deserve a last fling, I want to taste life first.'

He opened his arms wide to embrace all Allasol, and asked with furious wonder:

'Loyalties? To this shyster's paradise? To these potters of twopenny creams for sale at twenty times the price under an assumed name? Sleek! Nearness! Why, you *can't* . . .'

'Sleek's very good. *I* use it.'

'Loyalties! And what about our extra half-hours filched for lunch? What about your dentist? I'm your dentist, and my chair's in the Spinning Wheel, I'm the first dentist with a rocking-chair. *And* I'm your poor old grandmother you buried!' he shouted. 'Why, you'd cheat them soon as look at them!'

'Bun Stanbetter!'

'Look here, Sandra, you can stay for your lousy loyal little party here tonight and I'm going back to the Tropical Bughouse, but *what about tomorrow?* For heaven's sake, let's act *tomorrow*, if we can!'

'Don't shout.'

'I'll shout this lousy alchemist's den down all about my ears—'

'Some ears. Why don't you take off?'

Bun did not alter his tone, he still went on shouting:

'Which reminds me, there *is* another plane coming into service in January. I think we might be able to use it. It'll give us a better chance, a few days' breathing space. But only a few days, only a day or two!'

He had raised his finger and was shaking it at her.

She was furious.

'Why do all men shout?' she shouted.

'Why do all women think with their mouths? Talk, talk, talk—'

Icily she said:

'Because it's our only defence against being pushed round by great brutes like you.'

It made him feel awful—he knew it was old hat, but he felt himself grow big and clumsy, and this made him suddenly droop his shoulders, anything to make himself smaller.

'What's the matter, Bun—are you ill?'

Sorry for himself, he caught at it:

'Not too good—it's that stuff they shot in.'

'Oh darling.'

'It's all right.'

He shrugged his shoulders. He felt a cool new ascendancy.

'So that's that,' he said quietly. 'I see I'll have to wait. I'll have to go out there alone. To begin with.'

She was not deceived.

'Will you ring me tomorrow?' she asked.

'Can't I lift you home tonight?'

'Oh, darling—I don't know when we'll finish up here, and you've got to go back to what was it, the Tropical Medicine place? No. Tomorrow.'

He said slowly: 'You know, Sandra, I can't wait forever.'

'All right, all right,' she snapped. 'I'm not asking you to.'

'Right!' he shouted.

He turned sharply and banged open the fire-door. He did it with head in the air, a most formally cold exit.

'Goodnight,' he said.

'Bun, you can't go that way!' she said.

'Oh, can't I? The air's cleaner.'

He slammed the door, and she heard his footsteps ringing on the first flight of the iron staircase. She ran out. She suddenly thought: He really might be ill—tropical fever, and this damp cold air!

'Bun, darling!' she called, and started to follow him.

But she stood there bent forward and stuck. One slender heel had caught in the iron grid: she stood swaying and helpless.

A second only to reach down and get her foot from the shoe: another to wrench it free from the hole. But yet another to wonder if she could trust her stockinged feet on the cold, dirty iron—and by this time Bun's footsteps were far below, and though now she called again, 'Bun! Bun!' into the great dark well between the offices she still hesitated, and only heard like an echo the single word ring up to her:

'Nuts.'

Or could it have been 'night'?

Whatever—it was final. He could jolly well look after himself. She turned back flushed with injustice—at being shouted at because she had asked for a little time to think! Wasn't that what every woman asked for, with the man on his knees gently proposing? Gentle! Gentle my foot, she stormed, stamping short-stepped back into the corridor, slamming the door behind her.

She limped back to the office. Jill greeted her, swinging a bottle.

'A little of what you fancy?' she asked, her big pleated skirt swirling. 'Lost your boy again?'

'Who? Bun? He just called in.'

'Who? Bun?' Jill's flushed face mimicked, big watery blue eyes beaming. 'We thought you'd gone for good.'

Sandra put on a sour smile to cover the jump this gave her. But they didn't all think that? That she'd left Allasol? Then she remembered that of course Jill was in her confidence.

The word 'lost' lingered a moment. She never seriously thought she would lose Bun—only sometimes in moods of nervous insecurity. This was not one of them. She tossed back her glass—a thick Slovene Chablis—and narrowed her eyes:

'As you may know, Bun is not the only fish in the sea. What goes on here now?'

'Wow, it's a riot,' Jill giggled. 'But you mustn't talk about Bun like that!'

Sandra looked round. Bone and Bossom had gone off to entertain some other department. Sue Blair and Mark had also disappeared, it looked empty.

'Give me another drink,' she snapped.

Jill's eyes opened wider: 'I say, you *are* going it!'

'Where's the man-eating Susan Blair? Sunk back into her pool?'

The wine, and all it was mixed with, had begun to beat in her head. So she was going it? Then go it she would, she muttered to herself. She felt like singing and shouting blue murder at the same time.

'Sue? She's in H. J.'s room with Mark,' Jill said. 'You wouldn't believe it, I've just been in there with them and H. J. too. They were all looking at her photograph together. Did she turn a hair? My, she's a cool one. Stood there discussing herself with them just like a cucumber, I mean cool as a customer.'

Just then they all came out of the inner office, laughing together, glasses in their hands. Sandra walked pointedly away to where Mavis and Hearst were sitting perched by Mansford's desk. Mansford was still in his chair, strained and bleary-eyed.

'Mr Hearst, tiny one,' she laughed gaily, 'what exactly *have* you got on your mantelpiece?'

'Mantelpiece? What mantelpiece?'

'I shouldn't be here,' Mansford said to a little house of rubbers and pencil-stubs he had made on his blotter, 'I shouldn't honestly be here.'

'Your mantelpiece at home. I know about *yours*,' she said to Mavis, who had just taken a crème de menthe jelly to go with her ginger wine.

'The blue vase is nearly full of half-pennies,' Mavis said dreamily, without thinking, 'nearly full-right-up.' She then ate, casually, three potted shrimps from a carton there on the desk.

Hearst, who alone had taken nothing to drink, felt a small chill of terror. Were they clairvoyant? Behind the big picture of his old friend Colburn and his regiment, he kept a copy of *The Sunbathing Gazette*.

'Well,' said Sandra guessing, 'there's the old group photo to begin with. School, eh?'

Hearst stared at her.

Mansford was saying: 'But they don't like you waiting at the hospital. After all, all the fathers couldn't wait at the hospital all the time, could they? Where would the corridors be?'

'I don't know what you're talking about,' Hearst said stiffly to Sandra.

'Your mantelpiece!' Sandra laughed, and, starved of action, the wish to match-make suddenly came to her. She winked mischief into her face and sniggered:

'How would the things on your mantelpiece go on Mavis's mantelpiece? What do you think, Mavis?'

'His things on my man—?' Mavis began.

Hearst tried to recover:

'The little lady on my left has taken leave of absence off of her rocker.'

'Have his things on my mantelpiece?' said Mavis, 'Whatever next!'

Lucky guess? Hearst thought. Or did she know some-one who knew him—had she been nosing round? He himself had nosed down a few week-ends back to look at H. J.'s house, peering through the hedge and confirming his suspicion of riches. Now he put his hand to his heart and chanted to Mavis:

'How would Madam appreciate a genuine antique tobacco jar in the form of an elephant's foot? With a chip off the old toe-nail?'

Mavis coloured:

124

'Go on with you,' she said, looking down at her cardigans.

Sandra was away to other mantelpieces. Pointing at Ralph Mansford, she asked accusingly:

'And who's he?'

Mansford knocked over his little house of india-rubbers, as if he ought not to have made it.

'Me?' he said.

'The cat's grandmother,' Jill giggled.

'No, I mean who are we all?' Sandra said, pointing at them one after another—and now including H. J. and Monica who had come up with Sue and Mark behind.

These four were all laughing, looking in their more expensive clothes more like part of a cocktail party; yet they were only talking shop. '. . . it's a good product and a good campaign,' H. J. was saying, 'but we seem to have jimmied the sell-in somehow. How can we service the public that way?'

'You know where you can put it,' Mark laughed, 'up-the-market.'

H. J. belched quietly inside himself, swelling and subsiding, lips firmly pressed:

'No laughing matter, Mark,' he said. 'Service to the public's the Mission's first concern.'

'You don't say?' Hearst put in easily. Christmas comes but once a year and could be marked by a little free speech.

H. J. looked at him sharply:

'We've always said it, haven't we? And we mean it,' he added with emphasis.

'Other day,' said Hearst, 'I drove over—on a bus of

course—to a certain village not a hundred miles from Guildford and came across a fine half-timbered residence standing in its own grounds. My, I thought, chap who owns that's given some service to the public.'

'Guildford? What village?'

Hearst smiled to himself:

'Nice bit of service those fifteen bedrooms are, I thought. Trim stretch of gravel, too. And the lawn—the lawns, I was much enamoured of the lawns.'

'What are you getting at?' said H. J.

'Of course, you might say it's a service to the public to employ a couple of gardeners and a cook and so on. Service with a smile, I'd say.'

H. J. squared his shoulders grimly and turned away.

'Man must be drunk,' he muttered.

Hoping to ease things, and seeing the sweets on Hearst's desk, Monica broke into a peal of laughter. She also liked to see her Godfrey's assurance rattled.

Mavis was staring at Hearst in horror. She thought Monica's laugh was directed scornfully at H. J. And she suddenly boomed at the top of her voice:

'You pack of rotters!'

Everybody turned. The whole party rocked to a sudden stop. A silence, but for tinkling of glasses and a shifting of feet. One voice, Quentin's, went on in a corner:

'That boiler gives me my three baths an hour—idling at 180.'

Mavis was shaking with fury; but her shouting voice came cracked, low.

'The poor man's got to live, hasn't he?' she shouted. 'He's not here for his health, is he? Health,' she gave a hysterical sob, 'that's a good one! He works his fingers to the bone! And what do we do for him? What do I do for him? What *can* I?'

Everyone saw what is seldom noticed early enough— she was quite drunk. But on ginger wine? With her grey hair and cardigans and her big grey skirt, her spectacles and one leg bandaged beneath her stocking, she stood pathetically swaying—and very isolated. The space to either side of her seemed to grow greater, and she herself to shrink smaller.

She turned round on Monica:

'You're the trouble! Messalina!' she quavered, and burst into tears.

Sandra was over to her, putting her arm round the bowed shaking shoulders.

'There,' she whispered, 'there, there,' and slowly turned her away.

'Well!' Monica said loudly and with scorn.

Sandra turned: 'Shut up!'

H. J. murmured: 'Really, Miss Lee, I don't think you should—' but this was lost as everybody whispered one thing or another: 'A drop too much.' 'Ginger wine?' 'Poor old girl. . . .'

But Sandra was only listening to the shaking frail body she held, and to what Mavis now sobbed through a fist gripped at her mouth:

'. . . I love him . . . poor man . . . oh, why can't they let me . . .? I don't ask anything. . .'

'Come on,' said Sandra, 'we'll find somewhere quiet.'

She led her slowly out into the passage. Along by Reception stood a small room marked, for no reason, PRIVATE. Sandra tried the door, it was unlocked. The room was full of cartons. They were stacked all round the walls, but with one or two standing loose on the linoleum. She sat Mavis down on one of these.

'Now *that's* all over, Mavis,' she said. 'Don't you worry. They've all had too many drinks. No one's going to remember.'

'I've disgraced myself,' Mavis said quietly into her hands.

'Nonsense. You just sit here quietly and forget all about it.'

'I've disgraced myself,' Mavis said, 'and I'm a Cook.' And she began to sob again.

Sandra could only stand there and pat her shoulders, and think: All these years. Every morning on the same train towards this same bleak block of boxes where her devotion lay. And the big slob of a man quite unconscious of it.

She was deeply sorry for her. But there was nothing she could do—she could only wait until the tears were over.

Her eyes wandered over the brown cartons reaching nearly to the ceiling. It was difficult to read letters on them by the one weak yellow electric bulb. 'Moujik' one said. 'Muscovy Cossack' another. Red and white labels saying *Fragile* were pasted on at all angles. They looked dazzling after a while, like a dizzy abstract wallpaper.

The box under Mavis began to collapse. There was a

papery crunch of broken glass. A smell of scent rose round them. Sandra recognised Moujik. 'Fragile's right,' she said brightly. 'Now come on, Miss, we're going out and getting you washed and brushed up.'

There was a wet stain where Mavis had been sitting. A voice came through the door, H. J.'s, as he passed along the corridor:

'That man Hearst's certainly got a strange sense of humour—'

Sandra clapped her hands across Mavis's ears.

'If it wasn't Christmas, I'd sack—'

'And if he wasn't so useful at his job,' Monica said sharply. 'Where's that old fool Cook now?'

'Oh, she'll be all right,' his voice faded away down the passage.

Sandra opened the door, and hurried Mavis along to the Red Hell.

In that place, in the rose-reflected mirror, Mavis saw her face and shrieked, 'Oh, what a sight!' quickly losing her grief in a patting of hair and wiping of eyes. But to Sandra she had looked little different from usual.

'Would you think this was the same office?' she said for the sake of talking. 'Mavis, it's all a kind of dream really, everyone taking a drop too much, and tomorrow they'll all never believe it happened . . . if they even remember.'

'Oh no,' Mavis said quietly.

'And with Christmas on top! How could anyone remember this little do?' Sandra insisted through pouted lips as she put on lipstick.

'No,' Mavis said to the pink glass.

Together they patted and arranged themselves in that quietly echoing place. The smell of Moujik grew stronger every moment. There was no more to say, though Sandra went on trying to say it.

Then Mavis pointed to one of the closets.

'Now I'm just going in there to sit down quiet for a while.'

'Oh, you can't!' Sandra gasped.

'Thank you, dear,' Mavis smiled. 'I'm best in there for a bit. You run along now and enjoy yourself.'

Footsteps sounded outside, and she quickly went in and shut the door.

'Enjoy myself!' Sandra said, drawing her lips down, thinking of this little oldish woman sitting locked in there alone, 'as if I—'

Jill burst in, saw Sandra, and cried:

'I say, what a schemozzle—' before she caught Sandra jabbing her finger at the closet door.

Sandra said in a cheerful voice:

'Well, back to the fray!' and went out.

She was horrified to think what Mavis might hear in that resonant place with its thin cubicles—but as she closed the door the passage substituted for the smell of Moujik the strains of *Yours, Yours* ascending from the Pool. Her heart quickened to the sound of this, her song, and now after the first long line,

Yours, Yours,

there came up the extensive fluted notes of the second line,

I'm yours

130

and her whole body felt taller and stronger and more graceful. She looked back at the Powder Room, shrugged her shoulders—for what could one do, sit on guard?—hitched at herself, patted down her dress, and strode firmly along the corridor—to find the mailing clerk Bone all alone pouring eggy yellow Advocaat on those waxen hyacinths.

He was dripping a big yellow blob on each individual flower, where it hung or slobbered down like a libation of thick wet pollen. And now he was reaching high to the topmost hyacinth to complete his curious eggy errand.

'Why—whatever—?' gasped Sandra. 'A higher cynth I *never* saw!' she giggled.

Bone looked round amazed. His glistening face blanched big with fear and wonder to see Sandra there alone with him, talking to him. His face boiled with animal fat, his plastered hair seemed to stiffen on its scalp with youthful potency.

'B-b-bossom betted me I wouldn't do it,' he said.

'A higher—' she began to repeat, when she realised the light shining from Bone's bulging eyes, a light that said only one thing: 'And I would do it for *you* too, Sandra', and she remembered how Bone followed Bossom like a big hangdog shadow round the office, and saw herself in Bossom's place. All friendliness left her.

'You'll spoil those flowers,' she said severely. 'All that sticky stuff'll never come off.'

Bone looked at the flowers with horror.

'Oh, it'll w-wash,' he stammered and then looked at her again, straight, with beaming adoration.

'Like a drop?' he said, pointing the eggy bottle towards her.

The yellow stuff had dribbled over the top and down the side of the long stem to where it grew thick in Bone's ham grasp. Sandra shuddered.

'I must get on,' she said, and suddenly felt powerful enough to be kind. 'Bone, darling, I must be off,' she said.

Bone conferred dominance on people, Sandra had sucked strength from him and now went off along the passage revived and more sure of herself than ever. And Bone—Bone in his room alone at nights, or at moments set specially aside during the day to dream of it, Bone would remember for months that magical marvellous word, that 'darling'.

She walked now so fast, hammering on her tight-skirted heels that, turning the corner before reaching the office, she collided with a man's grey back, Ralph Mansford's. He was standing there stopped in thought on his way back from the men's lavatory—wondering about the telephone, whether the calls were really put through, whether he would ever, ever know. Sandra's body threw him a whole pace forward before she steadied him.

That moment's clutching touch, the unbalance, and then the relief drew a pleased laugh from their two faces suddenly so close together.

'Oh, it's you,' Mansford said happily. 'Near thing. Let's siddown.'

In this bend of the corridor, hidden from both office and main vestibule, someone had pinned up a display runner, one word in capital letters HAEMOGLOBIN. Under this they sat. A continuous rising chatter came from the nearby office.

'Shouldn't drive on the right, you know,' Mansford said puffing a weary sigh.

She laughed: 'I've got my third party—'

He put up a splayed hand right through his plastered black hair, raising it like shining separate feathers, and moaned:

'What about *my* little third party?' he said. 'Look—it's like this. Will the call come through or won't it? If I go in there by the telephone, they'll make me drink. But if I don't go in I won't hear the—'

'You can hear it from here,' Sandra said. 'I really know.' She nodded brightly at him, as at a doll or a child.

'Then let's have a drink,' he said, to make his point.

A half-empty bottle—Australian Tonic Wine—stood against the skirting board opposite, with a pink-dregged glass beside it. He filled the glass, sipped and handed it to Sandra.

'Loving cup,' he said.

Jill came past with Monica. Monica looked at them casually and went on. Jill hung back a second.

'Heard about Hearst?' she said. 'H. J.'s mad at him. Ructions!' and she went smiling on her way with a light, heady laugh.

Sandra took a great gulp of the wine.

'I say!' said Mansford.

'I needed it,' Sandra said darkly. 'So there's no news?'

He stared at her with wild white eyeballs. A look of terrible urgency twisted his handsome face. She suddenly saw that this was how he would look at her if he were in love, demented with love for her.

'No,' he grunted, ' and there she is, suffering and frightened, poor little thing. Oh, why should it happen to them so, who aren't strong enough even to carry a heavy suitcase? Yet this awful weight inside them?'

He clenched his hand round the bottle so that the knuckles showed pale bone, and poured another drink. He drank it all. 'It should be me,' he said, 'it should be men.'

'Now, Ralph,' she said brightly, 'women like it, really.'

He sat there staring hard at nothing.

She opened her eyes wide, and said to him:

'It's *natural*, Ralph.'

He looked all round the bare little corner of passage, grey paint everywhere, old gas-pipes and early electric fitments on the ceiling all painted over with matt grey paint.

'I love her so,' he said.

'I know,' Sandra said softly, and she thought of poor Mrs Mansford lying there sealed off in bed. And how freshly attractive Mansford himself looked! Always handsome, worry and loneliness tousled him—she wanted to take him in her arms.

'Think how proud you'll be,' she said brightly again, 'wheeling the pram on Sundays!'

Mansford's mouth fell open.

'Oh, you'll find life quite changed,' she said.

He looked more despondent than ever.

'What?' he said. 'How?'

134

'Well, all kinds of things happen! Babies are *fun*, Ralph! Like the first day baby walks. That's a great day, Ralph, when he gets up on his little toddlers for the first time.'

'That's when he begins to fall, isn't it?'

She laughed—but she had seen a new and desperate look in his eye. And her own lashes lowered.

'This little piggy went to market, this little piggy stayed at home—' she began to chant.

He caught her wrist and held it hard.

'Sandra, you're a dear good girl to stay and talk—but please don't, *please*.'

She put her free hand on his hand on her wrist, and kept it there. Her mouth held a wistful, intense expression —but she made her lips move round the words slowly and wetly:

'You'll have to settle down now, Ralph.'

Mansford was already settled down. Yet hearing this from Sandra's face so doomful and close, he felt himself vaguely to be some kind of freebooter tasting the last hours of liberty.

'Yes,' his throat whispered, 'yes.'

When suddenly she sprang up, but still clutching his hand.

'Heavens!' she said. 'I'd forgotten! Come with me— quick!'

She pulled Mansford the few steps along the corridor to that door marked PRIVATE where Mavis had sat. No one was in the passage. He was muddled, unhappy, and half drunk—it was easy.

135

'Mavis sat on the Moujik,' she explained, 'and I've got to see what the damage was. We could hide it up, couldn't we?'

'Mavis sat on the Moujik?' Ralph asked.

She opened the door and they went into a blanket of scent thick as furnace heat.

'I smell trouble,' he said, 'I smell a rat.'

'It was this one, I think,' Sandra said, bending down.

It was when their wives had babies that they were at their wildest, wasn't it? She looked up at him, raising her chin so that he could see the dimple between the tops of her breasts, and said:

'Heady, isn't it?'

Mansford's eyes lost their worry, and seemed to be thinking inwards. A shut door does something to a man. She straightened up and face to face they moved together at the same time, arms went round arms, and she had just time to murmur, 'Oh, Ralph,' before their mouths were met and were lost.

Feeling herself to be yielding, and yet pulling him to her—and then his lips were suddenly gone! She opened her eyes to see him staring down at her fixed in a terrible kind of wonder.

'No,' he said, 'no!'

Then he was bent down over the carton, tearing at it with his fingers, flapping up the two cardboard flaps, and being carefully, cleanly sick all over the smashed little bottles within.

He mumbled up at her through a handkerchief.

'Oh God, oh dear—I'm sorry—wine—' and feeling

how this must have looked, straight after the kiss, and perhaps knowing how it was his own shame that had sickened him, he repeated for her: 'The wine.'

She saw his eyes over the big white handkerchief like eyes over a sheikh's burnous. The worry, the wine, she thought, and put her arm round his bent shoulders to comfort him.

'Oh dear, what can I do with it?' he said, looking down at the neat mess; and his hand went down to close the two flaps. 'I can't carry it all to the—'

'Just put it in the corner,' she said.

'I can't throw all these bottles down the—' he said, and then clutched his handkerchief harder and mumbled: 'I think—I'm going to be—again.'

He rushed out and along the passage. Sandra bent down to push the carton against the wall. Her whole heart spun with joy and triumph. Something had happened! She had seduced a man who was in love with his wife, and that wife in labour with his child!

She felt thoroughly, gloriously wicked: superior to the wife, and curiously contemptuous of Bun. She was freed: and now, careless even of her own manners to herself, she sniffed the air above the carton, smelled only scent, and smiled.

'One up to Moujik', she said.

Mark Deane and Monica had found Sandra's scrapbook, which she had left out on her desk. To leave this secret love so openly abandoned was some measure of the strangeness of the day. They were chuckling with delight.

Monica pointed to a coloured photograph of Don Terry again, now in a white tuxedo and posed at the door of a thatched cottage among herbaceous borders a little taller than himself.

'What goes on in the girl's mind?' Monica sniggered.

'Oh Lord, look—a little corgi too, lost in the lupins.'

Monica suddenly looked serious, and said quietly:

'You know, there *is* something about these herbaceous bs.—corny maybe, but there's nothing more coloured. Bleed beautifully round a pack?'

'Over my dead body,' Mark said, and swiftly turned the page.

A double-spread, on glossy white paper, simply of one giant pair of female lips! Romantically sensual, every soft crack apparent, they looked like two enormous fat red worms playing Cupid's Bow.

'Christ!' said Monica. 'Can't you hear her—"Such clever photography"?'

'Hear her?' Mark said. 'I can *see* her. Quick! She's just come in again.'

But Monica clung on to the book as his hands tried to shut it, and purposefully she laughed louder than ever.

Tiny Hearst's big bulk stood ill at ease. The courage of his remarks to H. J. had wilted. He saw that this might easily lead to one of these long grey words hollow with dignity—demission, superannuation, resignation. Jill's watery blue eyes shone with pleasure as she tried to comfort him.

'He won't remember,' she said. 'Nobody does after a

do like this. Think of last year—how much can you remember? It's like a dream to me. Something that happened but didn't really.'

But Hearst remembered too much from the previous year. He thought: Perhaps because I don't drink. But if I don't drink, why do I get intoxicated like the others? By the others, in fact? It's bloody odd. It's bloody dangerous.

'What was the last thing he said?' he asked Jill once again.

Bone and Bossom were back. Like many who thought of the party as at last a release from Allasol's affairs, they were busily talking shop. Bossom was saying:

'Wake up, if you had your In-trays where your Outs is and your Outs instead of your Ins, you'd go straight up to the desk with your Ins, slam 'em down and sweep round in one motion, in *one* motion, see, and carry away your Outs. You've got to have your Ins on the right facing you.'

'I see,' said Bone.

'It'd halve the time! You carry your Ins in your right hand, see, and you face the desk dead front on, other way you're cross-legged—'

'I like it how it is.'

'Cherry ripe—what you got screwed on up there, you bleeding twirp?'

'I'm left-handed, Bossom.'

'Lord Davy Crock it! Is the world running with cripples?'

Alec Quentin stood with a grey-haired accountant whose face was shaped like a spade and seemed to have no features. This was A. E. Thomas, known as Taffy the Tax, and the man who had exchanged the dirty word 'expenses' to 'personal disbursements' and finally 'bursarials'.

Now he was expanding from his own province like Hearst, and giving Quentin a piece of Christmas mind. Quentin jigged about, eagerly catching his words like thrown nuts. Only he was really studying Taffy's complexion, wondering that a skin could be so grey.

'Of course,' said Taffy the Tax, 'it's none of my business, and I'm not one to poke my nose in, I like a man to keep placewise. But I had to boil over. You can check your sales campaign—but no one's ever sure what reaction the *names* of products have. So when young Mark wanted to call that confounded eye-pencil "Village Green", I—well, Quentin, I tell you as man to man, I couldn't take it. I reached a point tantamount to imbalance.'

'Really?' said Quentin, and thought: How would he look with a blue rinse?

Sandra swept in triumphant and flushed, feeling like a film-shot; feeling like the entrance of a big diamantée blonde with strong shoulders muscling fresh from the Powder Room to the party she would now galvanise, astronomise, blow star-high.

She crossed the threshold into what felt more and more like a real cocktail-party—a wall of smells and smoke and high-pitched chatter you had to push through. And in spite of the cold black glass of uncurtained windows, and of the work-a-day clothes of the people, and the charts on bare grey walls—there was the growing detritus of merriment, always more and more bottles and glasses and tissue paper, and Sandra now in any case saw it as she wanted to, a place to go gay in.

'Hi, Jill!' she shouted, as Jill was nearest.

Jill caught her arm to bring her instantly into mouth-melting conspiracy:

'Look, Sandra—do you think Tiny spoke out of turn?' she said. 'About Guildford—H. J.'s house and that?' she soughed up and down, consoling.

Sandra took in the anxiety in Hearst's eyes. His huge body in its baggy clothes seemed to have lost bulk—he stood uncertainly in clothes too big, awkward as a child accused of naughtiness.

Her flash of power needed someone to hit.

'It was a bit pointed, wasn't it?' she smiled.

Yet at the same time she was powerful enough to be generous.

'But it's a party after all,' she added. 'And H. J.'s got other worries. The bonus. And all this leather he goes on about—'

'What leather?' Hearst said, awed.

'Oh, an old company he's been gifted. Present from a dead cousin. Doesn't know what to do with it—worried it won't wear out or something. I've been re-typing one letter all week. Hey—isn't this a party? Where's my glass?'

Hearst began to think again. Best thing to do was to

do H. J. a good turn. 'Leather,' he thought. 'Durable leather—I see his point. I wonder now. . .?'

'A little of what you fancy?' Jill said to Sandra, and gave her a dirty glassful of Fortified Pineapple Cocktail.

Then she looked at Sandra more closely: 'I say, who's swallowed the canary?'

Sandra laughed, showing all teeth, brazen.

Jill looked quickly round. 'Where's Ralph? 'she said.

This was better! Sandra said in a slow straight-eyed way that she didn't know, meaning she did. Jill giggled.

But as with an orchestra this giggle was repeated by a brass of laughter from the direction of Sandra's desk, as Monica firmly turned the leaves of the scrap-book.

Sandra's chest squared and her breasts stuck out like pointed missiles, loaded and trained.

'Well of all the damned cheek!' she said loud, and went briskly over to Monica convulsed, Mark apprehensive.

Quentin was saying: 'Quite. Quite.

'Village Green?' said the spade-faced Taffy, 'Village Idiot, I said to him. Though he's the boss's nephew. And I'm not one to speak anti-turnwise. By the way—I heard Hearst blew his gaff with H. J. Does this mean a slight case of superannuation?'

'Oh yes,' Quentin said absently, still peering close at his skin. How would this curiously grey face look in the family circle, bathed in the cold blue glow of the television? For television blue and strip lighting were the cosmetic future; something had to be done about it.

A look of fear, a momentary grey glitter like mar-

quesite among the other greys, passed over the accountant's face:

'Gone too far?' he said. 'Have to go?'

'Oh yes,' Quentin said.

'Now, Bone, with *your* left hand and both our Ins and
Outs and therefore one of us cross-legged—we've still
got a five-and-a-half-day week, see? So one of us does
more, eh? I mean, you can't split a man down the middle.'

'No,' said Bone.

'So why not re-deploy your Ins and Outs to facilitate
your mail-collection proportionate to the hours of your
right-hander or your left-hander, whichever does his most
mail in your total week? See? You've got to get on and
think, Bone!' Bossom ended, stretching his arms wide
as a present to Bone.

Bone's heart bounded as he saw Sandra pass stamping
close by.

'Well—I dunno, Boss,' he said vaguely.

Bossom looked aghast at him.

'Kiss me,' he said. 'Kiss me—I want to—' burying his
face in his hands.

'Enjoying yourself?' said Sandra to Monica.

In her warpaint, her bright brown hair, green-daubed
eyes and fluorescent red lipstick, she stood panting and
looking bigger than usual. But not to Monica. She pretended not to notice in a fit of laughter.

'Oh, the niceness of it,' she hooted over her big tongue,
'oh, the blues are so bluey, the borzois so borzy, the—'

Sandra recognised the page with her favourite Venetia Vaduz stepping out in three blues, cerulean and midnight and heavenly, with a few borzois.

'What's wrong with V. V.?' she said sharp.

Monica opened all her teeth, laughing, her eyes closed in slits.

'Oh, Marge, don't you see? Who*ever* could this *marvellous* book belong to? It's the most heavenly, cretinous, prissy . . . oh!'—and her slit-eyes opened wide and her open mouth shut—'oh, it's not *yours*, is it, darling? I must be *château* bottled!'

'Give that here!' Sandra shouted. 'Who d'you think you are, peeking into other people's things?'

'Oh, Sandr-ah, we were only looking—'

'Been through my desk too, I suppose? I'll know if something's missing—'

'I say!' Mark said.

Monica drew herself up cold.

'I think you'll have to take that back, my girl.'

'I'll damn well take *this* back,' Sandra shouted, and grabbed at the book.

Monica's bag stood on the desk. The album knocked it over. A gold lipstick, tissues and papery things gushed out. A toothbrush slipped to the floor.

'Hello? Staying out the night?' Sandra asked.

'Really!'

'That the way the tart cooks?'

Then she saw a jewelled clasp half-hidden by the rubber pad under her typewriter. With a corner of the album she edged it deeper.

Monica never saw. She was bent down picking the other things up.

'Of all the clumsy great awkward—' she was saying, when there was a little pop; something had gone inside the immaculate charcoal tube. And now against the clean dark grey of her skirt a little length of cheap frilled pinkish-orange slip slid into the open. It was frayed, and had been mended.

'La-la!' said Sandra.

Monica lost her temper.

'You silly little slut,' she shouted at Sandra, 'I'll settle you for that. Where was it—Sarawak—you're sliding off to? You'll be slid off double quick now, my good girl.'

'Why is it, Monica,' said Sandra sweetly, 'that you always manage to put people's backs up so?'

The sight of that slip had purged her of anger. She felt just easy and strong. She even felt *sorry* for Monica. It was a warm, rosy feeling.

'I—I *what?*' stammered Monica, who prided herself on her ability to deal with people.

Mark's eyes winced as he saw Sandra take Monica's arm and heard her gently say:

'I know—it's horrid not to be popular, but we *can't* all be, can we? It's probably something—you know, something that happened when you were weeny, just as weeny as—'

'Take your hands *off* me!'

'Now, Monny, where's your heart?' said Sandra still sweet. 'Where's that little rock?'

Mark closed his eyes.

Just then H. J. came back into the room, wiping his forehead with a handkerchief, although there was no sweat there. Monica went straight over to him.

'I don't know, I don't know,' he was saying, 'there's Mansford retching outside the lavatory and the hyacinths in a dreadful state, and I go myself'—he prodded his chest—'*myself* down to get Bletch to come up with a cloth and of course there's no lift and no Bletch, only a strong smell of rum. Things are getting out of hand.'

Sandra shouted: 'Ralph's in the Red Hell, he wasn't being s—' and bit her tongue.

'What next,' grunted H. J.

'I'll tell you what,' Monica snapped. 'I've been insulted to my very face—'

He looked very tired, folds and crinkles of tiredness sagging where all was usually so square and strong.

'I don't know what I do this for,' he said. 'Give them an inch and they take an ell. I don't know why—every day of the year organising this whole damn shoot, and now there's the leather—what do I do it for, why do I *do* it?'

Hearst's lip began to curve in a little smile. He fearfully stopped it.

'I'll give you an ell,' Monica flared. 'I'll ask why you employ girls who as good as accuse me of being a thief? I'll ask you what you're going to do about *that*?'

'Now, let's get this straight,' H. J. said wanly, recognising a tone his wife had used before they had gone their own ways.

Sandra recognised it too, and she felt warmer and

warmer as this possessive tone rang over the office finally announcing the intimacy between the two of them.

'Now, Miss Naseby,' H. J. said, who never called her anything but Monica.

And Miss Naseby realised too. She looked suddenly frightened, then lowered her voice. But she continued to go on and on at him, until his eyes began slowly to roll.

Mark drew Sandra back.

'It makes you thirsty,' he said, and reached for a fair bottle of Margaux he had hidden behind a big grey duplicator. He filled two glasses.

'It's time to leave,' he said.

'Oh?' Sandra said. Was this an invitation? She watched her bright mysterious figure reflected with this elegant young man in the dark curtainless window—the two of them drinking out in the night, dream figures floating over the deep office well.

'Yes,' said Mark, 'get out before bloodflow. It's early yet, but already we've got Tiny due for the sack, Mavis in what one might call a state of leaving—'

'Oh, no she can't, she'll miss us all so—'

'—and our putative father retching his heart out in the lou. There's Bone—I saw him—gone mad with the hyacinths. And now Monica throwing caution to the winds, and what's gone on in the Pool nobody would dare suggest. No, get out while the going's good, I'd say.'

Not an invitation, then.

'Why, Mark, don't you think it's a nice party?' she said, glittering at him as if she was the party.

But Mark only threw his head back and laughed.

'Oh, "nice" is the word! And there's Jill—I don't know.' He shook his head.

'What's Jill done?'

'That's it. Nothing. You simply can't imagine *anything* happening to Jill. Yet she's a handsome creature—'

This cheered her. It could only imply that Sandra looked the type that anything could happen to.

'Yes,' said Mark, 'get out before the skin flies'.

But still he made no move to go.

Sandra said: 'I do declare you're enjoying yourself really, aren't you?'

It came across him that perhaps he was.

'God almighty!' he said horrified. 'It can't be true!'

'What can't? oh Lord!' said Sandra.

Standing in the doorway was a robust elderly woman dressed in violet, frilled and jewelled, and topped with a large tilted hat piled with berries and greenery. Straight from the December night, she had a distinctly summery look. She was now pointing a pink umbrella at H. J. and, repressing a hiccup, walked straight over to him.

'I always make a round of my gentlemen Christmas,' she said, smiling like a queen over two amiable chins.

H. J. dropped his mouth open. He let it hang there. He was tired.

'I don't think I have the honour of—' he began.

The lady held up her hand to stop him.

'I'll give you three guesses!' she laughed.

'I. Yes. Of course,' H. J. stammered.

'Of course me foot,' the lady said. 'You never set eyes

on me before. I'm Mrs Tovey that does round for you!'

Her bosom shook with laughter, the waved frills danced like bluebells.

H. J. said: 'What?'

'Every day of the year but Mondays I'm here on my number twenty-three seven sharp.'

'Oh. Oh, really? Er—give Mrs Tovey a drink,' said H. J. to Monica. 'You'll have a little drink with us, I know, Mrs Tovey.'

'I don't mind if I do,' she laughed, and began brushing the front of her blouse with her hands, up and down, as if it had suffered a fall of dust.

'What's good for the goose—' she said looking round angrily. 'It's Christmas, isn't it?' she asked H. J.

H. J. agreed. Monica handed her a glass and was about to pour from a bottle of Brown Ale, when the lady stopped her.

'I only take wine, thank you, dear.'

Mrs Tovey drank, raised her glass to H. J., drank again, and took a deep breath to begin to speak.

Hearst saw his chance. He stepped forward.

'Now, you come and take the weight off your—come and sit down, Mrs Tovey,' he said, taking her by the arm.

'Now, which one would you be?' said Mrs Tovey, settling herself. 'The old brown wooden job with the sweetbags, or the six-legger I can scarce get under? You're *not* the grey contemporary, I hope,' she accused.

'The old brown wooden job with sweetbags in the drawers,' Hearst said amiably, twittering his pale lashes at her.

'Then there's many a humbug I've knocked off you,' she said. 'And right here and now I'm going to make it up to you.'

She took out a bright half-crown from her bag and banged it down in front of him.

'Buy yourself some humbugs,' she said.

His passing thought was, 'I'm tired of humbugs.' But he just smiled and pushed the half-crown back to Mrs Tovey.

'I wouldn't dream—' he began.

She pushed the half-crown back.

'I'm not a thief,' she said fiercely. 'It's when you're mouth's full of dust and that, there's nothing like a sweet to clear you.'

Hearst laughed nervously and pushed the half-crown towards her.

She pushed it back to him.

'Huff you,' she said. 'Huff. Huff. Huff and blow your house down.'

'Well,' said H. J. on the other side of the room, 'it seems that our Bolshevik friend has his uses after all. What on earth are we going to do when he's finished with her?'

'A little of what you fancy, Mr Deane?' said Jill. She had found the Irish whiskey again. 'She looks a dear old soul.'

'I'm driving,' H. J. said. 'Much as I need it.'

Monica looked at him sharply:

'You said you were staying—' and stopped herself, saying instead: 'Well, I won't be at the wheel of the old

Southern Belle to Brighton-by-the-Sea, so you can give me one, Jill dear.'

'Soon as asked,' said Jill pouring. 'She might wash your hyacinths down, Mr Deane, now she's come.'

A gleam of hope smouldered in H. J.'s eye, and died: 'If that Hearst didn't monopolise her,' he grunted.

'Well now, what's the time?' he said looking round. He looked up at the electric clock: then shot out his wrist-watch and looked at that.

'Five o'clock already!' he said hopefully. 'Well, it's a very merry little show.'

Nobody seemed to notice.

'It's been a grand party,' he repeated.

A grey spade-shaped face occurred at his left shoulder: 'Smart idea of young Mark's, that Village Green,' it said, 'damned smart, if I may be permitted to say as much.'

Monica tossed back her drink, said something under her breath, and went off to the Red Hell to adjust her slip. Jill remembered Mavis sitting there—Monica might say anything in her hearing—and ran after her.

The telephone began to ring. It made a quiet buzz-buzz all alone on Mansford's empty desk. Nobody heard it. After a while, it stopped.

Alec Quentin had come over to Mark and Sandra.

'You quite got us going on your mantelpieces, young lady,' he was saying. 'Even old Taffy the Tax there, man of figures as he is, fixed Jill Jenkins with a couple of china shepherdesses and a netball cup.'

Mark murmured: 'We gave *you* a terrible little row of poison-blue bottles, and a chunk of oolite—'

'Nonsense. I'm married. Put it at two lalique hornbills and a gold clock that goes ping—'

Their wives! Sandra thought with rapture and distaste. That's another thing. . . .

'Ping,' piped Quentin and went on in exact Scottish tones: 'But there you have a whole fallacy. We don't have what we want, we have what we're given or borrow: what simply arrives round us. It's like that "Show me a man's books, and I'll tell you who he is." Rubbish!'

'It's purely figurative,' Mark said, 'the mantelpieces.'

Quentin pressed his lips together:

'I don't like symbols,' he said. 'Simplify to complicate, that's all they do. Signposts to error.'

'You are going it,' Mark said. 'Go on.'

Sandra tried frowning with gravity at these passages, turning her face from one to the other with a blank serious look, careful not to smile.

But she soon lost interest. Her eye wandered. She caught the glint of Monica's clasp hidden beneath her typewriter cushion. Looking to see no one saw, she edged her long oyster-tipped fingers towards it.

The telephone started to ring again.

Bossom said to Bone:

'Know what I'd do if I had these offices? Buy the building up. Tear it down. Put up a new one. Property, Bone—that's what. Make a darn sight more than working your guts out peddling piddling scent bottles.'

'Cor,' said Bone, saintly adoration shining out to join the halo of youthful grease. 'You couldn't do that, could you?'

Bossom looked at him with disgust.

Sandra whipped the clasp into her bag.

'Kiss me, I want to be sick,' said Bossom.

She spun round at him, heart in mouth. What did he know? How had he said that then? But of course—it was one of his terrible phrases. Heart beating fast, she rejoiced in her guilt.

'I don't mind if I do,' laughed Mrs Tovey, as Tiny poured her another glass of wine, 'my throat's like leather.'

Leather, thought Hearst. Improve the shining hour.

'When I say "leather" to you, Mrs Tovey,' he said twinkling, 'what springs first to mind?'

'Eh?'

'What do you think of first when you hear the word leather?'

Mrs Tovey looked at him suspiciously.

'Men,' she muttered hoarsely, meaning to add: 'They're all the same.'

Hearst's eyes popped out of their lashes. For a second they stared like blue diamonds.

'Bingo!' he shouted. 'Got it in one!' He banged his fist down so the half-crown between them gave a troubled jump.

Mrs Tovey drew back, pressing her glass to her bosom.

'You've opened the dam, Mrs Tee, you've set the clock ticking! Containers! Permanent containers for replace-able Male Toiletries, Mrs Tee!' Hearst whispered, his whole big face transformed with craft and joy. 'Bottles of Vintage Aftershave, of Worsted Cologne! Tins of Duke Igor Talc! All held in classy stitched coach-leather permanent slip-ins! It's a gift!'

'Slip-ins?' said Mrs Tovey drawing back.

In the ladies' Hell, Monica was pinning up the strap of her slip. Jill came rushing in. Her anxious face, already flushed pink from running, turned many shades darker as the red walls had their way.

'Hello, Jill,' Monica said with a safety pin in her teeth, 'there's many a slip, as they say.'

'It's quiet down here', Monica sang. 'Thought at least that poor Mavis'd be hanging around.'

Jill stretched her mouth into a huge shushing shape.

'Something wrong with your teeth?' Monica asked.

'But that poor dotty old Cook,' she went on to the mirror, 'the cheek of her, imagining H. J. would—'

She was muffled to a stop as Jill's big scrubbed hand came across her mouth.

'Hey—oo—wassa?'

But Jill held on hard, in the pink mirror their twined bodies looked indeed like a representation from hell, ladies in torment photographed on a pink-tinted postcard.

A noise between a cough and a sob sounded from behind a closed closet door. Then, as if to suggest polite presence, a chain was pulled.

'Symbols!' Quentin was saying. 'Take the figure of Justice, the lady in the nightgown with the scales. What do weighing scales really suggest to the world? Nothing but Short Measure.'

'It's about what you get,' said Mark.

'But it's not what's intended. And what about a sack of coins—do you read greed or wealth?'

'A clash of symbols indeed. Sorry.'

Sandra moved away, swaying more than usually at the hip. That clasp now safely in her bag warmed her with an elegance of sin. She let a deprecating sneer droop the ends of her rouged mouth: this was directed not only at Monica the victim, but also at herself, victim of dark passions. Thief of diamonds! She stepped into the low white automobile and raced off down the gleaming coast-road, while he leaned towards her, moonlight rinsing his red tuxedo: 'Next stop, Monte,' he whispered.

She passed the telephone as it began to ring for the third time. She thought, Ralph! How'll we get him out of the Hell? and picked it up.

Wrasse's voice came from a long way away:

'May I speak to Miss Lee?'

And now Nevile!

'Miss Lee?' she said.

'Yes, Lee,' he repeated.

Silence. She held the receiver away. Men—she had them on a string, like beads. But what could he want?

'Hello,' she said.

'Sandra?'

'Yes.'

'This is Nevile.'

'Oh, hello Nevile.'

'You sound miles away, it must be the telephone.'

'I expect it's the line. You sound miles away too.'

'As a matter of fact, I am miles away. I'm at Hainault.'

'Really?'

'Yes. Awful bore—a bashed fender at Hainault! Can you imagine it?'

He laughed.

'But I'll be raring home at seven', he said. 'Can you anything till seven?'

'I'm not exactly at a loose end.'

'Sorry, I didn't mean that. How's the party by the way?'

'Kicks.'

'Oh, Sandra, I'm so longing to see you! I simply can't wait—'

'Well, if you're at Hainault, you'll have to,' she said sharply.

Can't wait what for? she thought. Something a bit too possessive about that Nevile.

'Have a heart, San,' he said. 'See you at seven then?'

'All right. About seven.'

'Have fun.'

'I'm seeing to it,' she said.

'I had a good afternoon too,' he said. 'Didn't tell you about a new line we're putting out, Toby Jugs with blondey heads and a couple of bosoms like sphinxes. Thought it up myself, if I may say so. Going like hot cakes.'

Just because she said she was having fun, did he have to cap it?

'Sorry,' she said. 'I must go.'

'Two dozen I got rid of,' he said.

'Bye-de-bye,' she said and rang off.

He was as yet far off. And careful small matters, like saying 'about seven' instead of 'seven', kept her ascendancy over him.

She let him take his place again as an idea, as the dark paramour enraptured, and with the remembered taste of Ralph Mansford's lips and the clasp in her bag, all her sense of dangerous innuendo was stimulated—and a cool, masterful thought occurred to her. This was the moment to ring Bun and tell him she loved him! Without pausing she picked up the telephone and began dialling.

It would underline everything—the calm double-faced statement. Yet was this in itself an unconscious wish for protection?

A woman answered.

No, Mr Stanbetter was not in his room. Wait—there was a message. He had gone to the Centre for Tropical Diseases, Mountjoy Street. If his doctor phones, he would be there till half-past nine. Was she his doctor?

'No, I'm the gas inspector,' she said, furious, and hung up.

And who were these women in Bun's rooming-house? She had seen one or two skulking in their house-coats to the bathroom—it all had an unsavoury note. And there he was out, carrying casually on, after their words together.

'You don't *look* like a gas inspector,' said Mrs Tovey chattily, handing her a glass of port. 'Tell me dear, is that big man I was talking to up the pole?'

H. J.'s hand was on Hearst's back, he was smiling and

strong again, the lines and little folds on his face had tightened up into thick red congenial muscle.

'I think you've got it, man!' he laughed.

'It also means,' said Hearst, 'no new staff for the stuff, no new organisational expense. You can channel the stuff through all your present contacts—same salesmen, same retailers. Put the stuff up-the-market too—strictly A class outlets.'

'Fine, fine,' H. J. laughed. 'Fine.'

But the last 'fine' tapered off, the slapping hand gave a last little pat of a different kind, and flicked away as if Heart's shoulder had turned sticky. Ridiculous to let the man take all the credit! His chin jutted out and his big capable boxer's forehead grizzled into a frown:

'Well,' he said, 'it's something to go on at least. It's given us a line to explore. An avenue.'

'Hand-sewn,' Hearst went on innocently.

H. J. gave him a look far fiercer than any he would have dared when he had been legitimately annoyed with him a quarter-hour earlier.

Taffy the Tax happened to catch this glance, and hurried from the room in dismay.

Bun's being out had disturbed Sandra.

'Yes,' she said and, 'No', as Mrs Tovey prattled on.

The Centre for Tropical Medicine was a safe place for him to be: but it made him unavailable, and availability was one of Bun's qualities. Moreover, that female voice on the telephone coloured the matter—though she knew very well it was simply a lodger, it was not a nice atmosphere, another girl knowing more about Bun than she. She sat there now thoroughly insecure: she took out a mirror and began dabbing at her face.

The sight of her eyes, greyish and immaculately dressed with their rings of kohl, mascara and green shadowgrease, absorbed and reassured her. So that when Bone now came over with a glass in his hand and said: 'I thought you might like a glass of sherry, Miss Lee,' she turned on him so blank and superior a glance that Bone nearly dropped the glass, as his heart fell.

He knew this look very well. It was a well-known glance he knew from many a fifteen-year-old, with all the cruelty of someone old enough to be in the game, yet too young for pity or grace.

'I'm sorry,' he stammered, looking away and saying it straight into H. J.'s face, who himself had been turning away from Hearst.

'What have you got to be sorry about?' H. J. asked sternly. 'A lad your age doesn't want to go about being sorry,' he smiled.

'No, sir,' Bone said miserably.

He doesn't know what trouble is, H. J. thought. He didn't have Hearst stealing his thunder. He doesn't have Warble Fly. And what other imponderables lie waiting, terrible things you hear of and never know when they might come your way—metal-fatigue, greasy heel, hard pad. And that awful thing sheep get—pulpy kidney?

The telephone began to ring again.

'Let's see you answer it, lad,' H. J. said jovially, as at a prize boy.

But Mrs Tovey's ringed hand had reached out, she gave a huge swallow to indicate the little joker dancing inside her, picked up the receiver, and in a drawling voice said:

'Gas Department!'

'It's not, it's secretariat!' Bone said brightly.

Mrs Tovey was saying startled:

'Oh! oh, I'll see—'

She clapped her hand on the receiver and hissed in a throaty whisper to Sandra:

'They want a Mr Mansford, it's a hospital—'

Sandra grabbed the telephone: 'I'll get Mr Mansford immediately—can you hold?'

A voice said: 'We've been trying this number for some time. It's very urgent.'

'Yes,' said Sandra. 'Hold on, yes!'

She jumped up and said loudly to everyone:

'It's the hospital! News at last!' and ran for the passage.

Jill and Monica were coming out of Red Hell.

'I'm awfully sorry, Monny, I had to warn you though, didn't I?' Jill was saying, in her plaintive placid tone, 'I really *had* to.'

'You didn't have to use judo, did you? My *hair*!' Monica said.

'It looks lovely,' Jill said.

'Who's speaking?' Monica snapped.

Sandra came running along in her tight skirt like someone kicked from behind.

'Quick Jill, quick!' she shouted, 'there's news for Ralph! Help me!'

For even at that time she felt she could not go alone into the Men's: somehow two of them made a difference.

'Heavens!' Jill said, as she was swung away.

'I hope for his sake', Monica muttered, 'it's not a girl.'

'Heavens, what if he's passed out?' Sandra said to Jill.

'Locked in a closet!' Jill breathed thinking how, calves braced and shoulder like a man's, she would break down that door.

But most gingerly they pushed open the door of the Men's: and with bent forward bodies, with feet carefully kept outside, as if behind the service line of a tennis court, called:

'Ralph Mansford! Ralph!'

Ralph spun round from the mirror, caught in the embarrassing act of looking at himself.

'No!' he said, 'No, it's not——?'

'Yes,' they cried joyfully.

'Oh God,' he said.

'Quick, Dad, quick!'

Their two faces laughing, all teeth and eyes and hungry girlhood, flushed and painted and brilliant—he winced to see himself now the centre of a worn traditional joke, like crossing the line at the Equator.

But their excitement infected him, he came jumping towards the door, still holding the towel in his hand . . . oh relief that it was over, oh wonder at what it would be, oh love for his wife smiling from the white pillow.

They chased along the passage, and round the last bend into the office. Everyone now knew and he was greeted with laughter and clapping. Cries of 'Come on, Daddy!' and 'Look out, it's twins!' and he raced to the telephone.

Bossom whisked the towel out of his hand, his quick eyes found a safety-pin among paper-clips on the desk, and with professional joker's delight he quickly had the towel round Mansford's thigh and pinned it.

'His first nappy!' he shouted.

More laughter, so that Mansford had to hold up his hand for quiet.

'Yes, this is Mr Mansford . . . oh . . . matron . . . yes . . . I'll hold on . . .'

He had one hand on the pinned towel and was laughing back at them, with a finger up to his lips shushing for quiet. Hearst suddenly fished out a pad:

'Quickski, let's make a book. Boy or girl?'

Mark got up on a chair behind him:

'Five to one the babe's a boy!' he shouted, and down to Hearst. 'Two heads are better than one.'

'Don't be macabre,' Monica said, and Mrs Tovey rocked like a coloured jelly, all her berries dancing.

Ralph said: 'Yes . . . this is Mr Mansford. Yes, matron . . . yes . . . oh . . . .'

And a long silence as his face drained white and the strength drooped from his shoulders.

'Yes . . . I understand . . . I'll be along at once.'

No one was laughing now. Bossom picked furtively at the nappy hanging askew on one grey-trousered leg.

Mansford put the telephone down.

But still Jill's voice cut through cheerfully.

'What—what is it?' she asked.

Ralph looked at her dazed. His tongue worked along his lower lip.

'A little girl,' he said.

H. J. took him by the arm. He said quietly, 'You don't look too good . . . come along . . .'

Ralph looked shyly round from one to the other. There was something humble in his voice, as if he did not want to bother them.

'My wife's dead,' he said.

'Come along, old fellow,' H. J. said.

He shook himself free of H. J.'s hand. 'It's all right. Thanks. I've got to go.'

As he was going he suddenly turned looking for something.

'You . . .' he said to Sandra quietly, 'the carton—all over Christmas . . .'

H. J. said: 'I'll come along with you.'

'No. I'd rather—'

'I'll drive you,' H. J. said.

'No.'

Ralph turned. So much authority in his quietness, in his isolated sorrow. H. J.'s hand dropped. He let Ralph go. And then at a decent distance, followed.

A brighter, harder light seemed to shine, soberly showing up the debris of a room as if after, not during, a party. No one knew what to say. Yet only words could help. And one after another they came: 'How dreadful.' 'Poor man.' 'What is he going to do . . .?'

VII

SANDRA stared down at the stretch of grey carpet by her shoes. Her whole inside throbbed empty with horror: not at what he had said to her, but horror of how suddenly things could really happen to you, of the danger of everything. She whispered silently for Bun. How could she have quarrelled? How could she have turned him away? Where now, how quick, how soon could she . . .?

People glanced at the door, at the black windows blank with night and the reflected room outside. It seemed one should leave—yet nobody moved to go.

Then a glass clinked, a drink was poured. Not a convivial drink, but a stiffener. And more words came, for now this thing had to be talked into perspective, and gradually glasses were filled again.

'How long had the hospital been trying to phone?'

'Was the line in order? Wasn't Sandra using it?'

'A man with a baby—what would he do?'

'He's got a sister living out Norbury way,' Hearst said, 'but it's Christmas, and people go away.'

'What did he mean, Sandra, by "carton"?'

Sandra swallowed: 'Oh, that. I don't know—he was upset. . . .'

People tried to remember anything they had heard of Mansford's home life, chance remarks of his—repainting a ceiling with a roller, a game of golf at Richmond, his wife lost in a super-market with somebody else's tray . . .

but no real picture came. Again that mysterious 'other' life, the unreal dormitory between office hours.

One drink followed another. Also, the time was half-past five, time of crowded trains and buses, and for once in the year most people at Allasol had sworn themselves a holiday from this battering rush-hour.

And the tragedy seemed to bind them to the room as to a duty, as if all hands must be available. So that now when Sandra said she was going, to Bun and the Tropical Medicine Centre, Jill cried in astonishment: 'But you can't go *now*, not at a time like this!' and never wondered why she said it.

H. J. came back.

'I had to let him go. Seemed to want it. Seemed all right. Monica, get his home number, will you? May be someone there—take it in my room—'

He turned to Sandra: 'But *is* he all right? I thought he was ill, before?'

'I don't know,' Sandra said quickly.

'I thought it was you who said he was in the toilet?'

She shook her head:

'Someone told me,' she said, 'someone did'—and then she caught Jill's eyes on her, their frank wide-open lids for once a trifle lowered.

H. J. nodded, dissatisfied, and abruptly turned to Quentin:

'He'll be away after Christmas. Someone else'll have to look after that Longeur survey.'

'That can wait,' Quentin said impatiently.

Sandra thought she could edge away. But to go now

would look like an admission of guilt. O heavens, why do we court disaster, she thought, when it's waiting round the corner to crash down from nowhere? Why do I always want to stir things up? She took up a glass and drank it off. Better, a bit. She poured another, and drank half this. The act of drinking made her feel daring, so did the drink.

'I say, aren't you going it?' Jill said.

'Not yet,' Sandra said. 'Why ever should *I* go?'

'I didn't say—'

'I don't know why you should think—'

'Anyway, you did say you were going just now.'

'Me?' Sandra gave a loud laugh.

It was the first laugh since Mansford's news, and it cut the room like a sharp bell. Everyone turned. Even Mark's eyebrows were raised. Mrs Tovey looked at her severely:

'Nobody thinks of that poor woman,' she said, 'nobody thinks of her that's given up the struggle.' And this was true; it was easier to pity the bereaved than the deceased: and of course Mansford was familiar to them all, except Mrs Tovey.

Sandra's laugh, however frowned upon, did in fact break the immediate tension. And Bossom, thinking more of covering his disastrous move with that towel, picked up a bottle of liqueur, an opened Christmas present shaped in glass like the Venus de Milo, and grimaced at it with his professional monkey-lip:

'Well I'll be bound—as the bishop said to the five-egg omelette.'

Monica was just coming out from her glass vestibule.

'Why don't you make yourself scarce,' she snapped at him. 'Haven't you got any friends down below?'

Bossom acted a mock look of terror.

'There's no answer from his home,' she said to H. J.

There was a sudden smell of Moujik.

As she came in, Mavis looked at nobody but went straight to her desk and began picking up her present parcels. She reached her cardigan from a hanger. Sandra saw this, the last drinks had confused her, and now they turned to sudden compassion for Mavis. She hurried over: 'Oh, Mavis, you're not going?'

'I am,' said Miss Cook very quietly, 'and I'm not coming back.'

'But you don't know what's happened!'

Mavis's eyes were tired and cold: 'I know exactly what's happened,' she said gravely. 'I'm not wanted here any more.'

'No, You *don't* know! It's Ralph's wife! She's dea— he's lost her.'

'I heard what Monica said while I was sitting in there. An old fool, am I? I expect it's what you all think,' she said, piling her presents into the big embroidered bag. Her sand-coloured cardigan greyed the skin on her neck, strands of grey hair had caught in the wool. Then she looked up startled: '*What* was that you said?'

'Ralph's wife—she's passed on.'

Mavis's face screwed up and she caught at her side as if at a thrust of pain.

'Oh, poor man—-poor woman. Where is he?'

'He's gone.'

Sandra told her what had happened. Partly to take Mavis out of herself, she told it with excitement; yet the telling itself was exciting too. Mavis saw this, watched her mouth widening with pleasure. Her eyes hardened.

'Then there's nothing to be done, is there?' she said. 'Except one thing—why don't *you* go off and marry that man of yours instead of gadding about and spoiling yourself?'

'Why—Mavis!'

'You aren't really the type.'

Being told this was worse than knowing it herself. Did everyone know? How could she know? She felt all the make-up wash off her face and flared back:

'If *that's* all you've got to say!'

Mavis smiled, but her eyes still had the stern, matron's brilliance:

'I mean it for your good, Sandra—we've been good friends, and I shan't be seeing you again.'

Sandra suddenly began to cry. She stiffened her mouth, but her eyes poured tears:

'Oh, Mavis, you can't go—you'll miss the office, with only your room to go to—'

'I love my room, thank you,' Mavis said quickly. 'You wouldn't know how I love the quietness. And how neat I keep it. And my linen. And it's orderly and clean and I don't know why people all look down on a bedsitter, for it's comfort that counts and more, it's *mine*, and you can keep all your excitements—'

'Please, Mavis, yes—'

'They all run it down, I've read it all in your magazines

and your highfaluting novels—run down library books and buns and prunes and custard and make it sound like cold mutton, and there I go too, I *like* cold mutton, what's *wrong* with cold mutton I'd like to know?'

'Nothing,' Hearst put in, putting out his stomach at them, 'with the aid of a well-chosen pickle.'

Mavis threw the last parcel into her bag. 'Pickles my eye,' she said, 'that's just what I *don't* mean!'

Sandra whispered up to him: 'She's leaving.'

'Me too by the look of it,' Hearst said, shaking his head in H. J.'s direction.

'You don't need to whisper,' Mavis said.

'Now what's all this, my good woman?' Hearst began to banter. Then he spoke lower, concerned and kind:

'Listen, Mavis, everyone's loco tonight. Give it another thought. Remember, you're my only support now Ralph's gone.'

He went on, now whispering, with Mavis pretending to look sour but already feeling better, better for this little resumption of the ordinary office atmosphere.

And Sandra had time to remember 'You aren't really the type,' and felt low again. She walked away and found a half-filled glass of red wine, saw dark grains of ash floating on top, shrugged, and drank it. The drink, and the rakish look of the ash, cheered her. 'What the hell does she mean, marry him,' she muttered. 'And die off with a baby?'

She looked round at what now seemed the dregs of a party. It must be all over, this dreadful little get-together: and over, a long time ago, the elation of those few

minutes before Ralph had his terrible news. She was sad
for them all and sad for herself and now not a little drunk.
I've got a hard head, she told herself, but this has been
going on far too long. I'm woozy. Mustn't get too
woozy with that Nevile on the horizon, if he's still on it—
big pillared portico of unknown house, winter-brown
pavements, street lamps hidden in mist and black twigs.
Only got hard head because won't loosen up, she thought
—who said that? Why, hard-eyed healthy pale medical
student, yes, at same dance with Nevile Wrasse. Because
of self-preservation, he said, because afraid of losing
control and anyway because may be the type that gets a
little hangover five minutes after each drink, he said.

And then she thought of all the parties and all the
dances when, blessed with good looks and painted to kill,
she had shrunk within herself and only envied others. And
the feeling she could never understand—how dancing
herself, even with a favourite partner, was never like the
look of another couple gliding in blissful circles to the
coloured music, taking part never came up to what
others looked like: their hearts aglow in their breasts,
hers in her mouth.

'Huh,' she said aloud, to coarsen away such thoughts,
'time to go. And time to have just one more drink.'

And as she walked to where a bottle stood between Jill
and Mark, half of her was in fact destined for Bun—she
could see herself sitting in the Tropical Centre waiting-
room—and half for the dark portico of Nevile Wrasse,
outside which stood the low-moulded sports-car.

The impact of Ralph's news had already blurred, it

seemed to have happened a very long time ago. It could quickly be recalled with an effort—and it needed concentration.

But at least two people had been reminded of their own homes because of Ralph's, and as Sandra passed Quentin she heard him saying: 'Only half an acre, my missus keeps turkeys . . . .' And she noticed with surprise that he was talking to more Production men who had come in with new bottles. Was the party then not over? And there was the sound of *Yours, Yours* again from along the passage, as if the Pool had come nearer. Or did it only sound so because the office here was quieter?

Mark was saying to Jill:

'Two rooms and a bath, that's all I need . . .' when Sandra snatched up the bottle that stood between them, drank off another glass of Pineapple Fortified, and said:

'I'll tell you a little story, there was this girl friend of mine who got drunk, drank too much.'

She stopped and pointed at Jill.

'Not her,' she said to Mark. 'I've never even told *you* this one,' she said to Jill.

'Never never never,' as the feeling to tell spilled over inside her, 'and this little girl had never got drunk before, not so much, and she'd never been in love before, not really fallen, and one night when they went dancing, oh it was after a wedding and that always upsets a girl in more ways then one—well, she was given too much to drink all afternoon and evening and when this boy said come and have a last drink up at my place she said yes. And so she went up to his little room.'

She looked hard to see Jill and Mark close, their faces were blurring. Tears were welling over her eyes—was it the drink? She hardened her mouth into a scornful smile. Mark and Jill were both staring at her wide-eyed. She giggled, and went on, but the tears would not stop.

'Crabby little room, all basins and wardrobes. And this little girl looked like a real princess in her lovely dance-dress. And she took a drink and sat on the bed and I think—' and she frowned hard now—'I think they kissed. Yes, that's it. They kissed.

'And the next moment, nice and gently, sweet and low, she passed out. There in her lovely dress, with Conrad leaning over her—yes, his name was Conrad, that was the boy's name, *Conrad*, I ask you—she went slap out.

'The next thing she knew was waking up in the morning. It was the first time anything like this had happened to her—you know, the room, a man. She didn't know where she was and then with a dreadful headache of a bump she knew. She looked round terrified—but, you know, kind of glad too.

'She was in the bed, in her underclothes, all of them, and alone. On the floor was a mattress—somebody had been sleeping there. But no Conrad. Only a note—to say try and leave quietly because of the landlady and then the words, "Don't worry."

'Don't worry! By that time, she knew she didn't have to. All night, all alone there! And he had played the gentleman!

'My God,' Sandra raised her face to them, shining

now with tears, 'she didn't know whether to laugh or cry!'

Mark thought: That's the third case of tears in half an hour, I really must get along.

'Never trust a man called Conrad,' he said.

'Who? Me?' Sandra said quickly. 'I never said it was me!'

Jill put her arm round her:

'You are a funny girl,' she whispered.

'I never said you did say—' Mark began and left off.

Sandra turned quickly away to her desk. Thrumming with tears, pleasure, shock at giving herself away— wishing to hide her face and see it at the same time, she took out a mirror and began stroking her cheek with cotton-wool. What would they think now?

Then past the mirror she saw a package lying in her drawer, Mummy's transistor! It was such a lovely little thing, gold and black, neat as neat, down payment as a present and Mummy to pay the rest. If she put it on very quietly? Surely Mummy wouldn't mind?

She finished her face, and took the shining box out of its bag. She stood it on a box-file, and turned the switch. How small it looked beside the big typewriter!

'The dulcet tones of their rendition of Jingle Bells,' said a confidential voice with a pipe in its mouth, 'and this is Jerry Carew giving you—Larry, Morrie and Rita! I think you'll like them. *I* do.'

Then there came a machine slamming of washboard music and wailing voices that sounded as if they were lost in a large, echoing cave, Jingle Jingle Jingle they wailed, evidently to find their way out.

The rich electrical sound of this music, together with now a wonderful relief that she had got that story off her chest at last, made her feel better; and she began to hum as she painted.

'Have you seen it?' Monica said abruptly above her. 'My clasp? It must have fallen out of my bag here.'

Sandra went on humming and painting, suddenly tense and cool.

'Did you hear me? My clasp must have fallen out of my bag,' Monica said louder.

'Be with you in a minute,' Sandra mouthed, raising her eyebrows to concentrate.

Monica made a deep breathy sound of impatience and snatched up the transistor.

'Hey,' shouted Sandra, 'leave that alone!'

'If some people have no manners, others have to take things into their own hands.'

'You're not taking Mummy's transistor in *yours*, not if I—'

She had her hands on it too. Oyster and coral nails battled over the glittering black box.

'I was only looking underneath,' Monica said, 'and anyhow, should you be playing it just now, after Ralph? Isn't it rather—thick-skinned?'

'You just let go this set!' Sandra said through clenched teeth.

For a moment their eyes stared hard into each other: Monica let go.

174

'And talking of thick skins,' Sandra panted, 'what's that layer of suet all over your face? I could lose myself for days in those pores.'

'Thank you,' Monica softened her voice to a cold equable tone. 'Now what I want is my clasp. Have you seen it?'

'No,' said Sandra.

'Then it's plain I must go on looking.'

'Plain's the word.'

'Really, Sandra, I don't know what's got into you. A glass too much, I should think.'

'You come over here with your home truths, you'll get some back.'

Sandra put the transistor back on its box-file. But she switched it off. Now she stretched her hands wide.

'Go ahead, look!' she said, and Monica bent over looking everywhere.

'Go ahead, I don't mind,' Sandra repeated standing back from the desk. She raised her eyes to the ceiling as though talking to an idiot.

Monica leant her hand on the keys of the big type-writer, the carriage shot like a battering ram and with a little yelp of its bell knocked the transistor off onto the floor. One of the gold knobs rolled off on its own, like a coin on an errand.

'You clumsy great ass!' shrieked Sandra, picking it up. Glass was smashed in one of its dials: a corner of plastic suède was ripped.

'Oh! You've broken it!'

'You upset my bag,' Monica said quick.

H. J. had noticed Monica's excitement from across the room, it looked dangerous—and he was there to pacify, anything for a quiet life.

'Now, girls, what's this?' he said jovially.

'She's smashed my transistor, that's what, and it's not mine, it's a present.'

H. J. put on a slow pontifical voice:

'A present to *you?* Or to *whom?*'

Divert them, H. J. thought.

'For my mother,' Sandra said, in fact cooling.

'You know, Sandra,' H. J. said, 'accidents will happen. My, it *is* a nice little job too. Yes . . . a pity! However—'

But Monica snapped in:

'She upset my bag: and I've lost that clasp.'

'Oh?' H. J. said, nodding judiciously.

'The *diamond* clasp!' Monica let out. 'You know. Clean vanished!'

H. J.'s face fell open.

'What?' he said sharply, 'You haven't lost that clasp I—' before he shut his mouth up so tight the lips quite disappeared.

Sandra heard, and so did Jill. They exchanged a quick glance. H. J. noticed it. So he told, at a speed calculated to appear casual, a cool lie:

'First things first,' he said to Sandra, 'I happen to know the people that make this set of yours. I don't think I'll find much difficulty in getting a replacement—if you'll allow me?'

'What, before Christmas?' Sandra demanded before she could stop herself.

'That's perhaps a little too much to expect. Present it in spirit,' he tried to twinkle, 'and let the body follow later.' Not bad. It rather pleased him.

'And second things second,' Monica snapped, *what about my clasp?*'

'It's not paste then?' Jill asked sweetly.

Sandra was thinking of her mother's reasonability, her bright understanding, which would be harder to bear than any rebuke. But she thrilled with wonder at Jill's acumen. Yet Monica was up to the mark:

'Just a *clasp*, dear? Of course not.'

She pulled straight her jacket, smoothed a hand across the brow of dark red hair, and added sharply:

'So we must all look! Get everybody!'

Sandra suddenly saw that if the clasp was made of real diamonds, then it would indeed be a serious matter if she were found out. At all costs she must not draw attention to her own bag. No whitened knuckles on the handle, she thought desperately, and don't look down at it. To keep her eyes up she fixed them in a goggled open glaze at nothing, so that Jill, remembering how quickly she had been drinking, whispered:

'Are you all right, San?'

Sandra nodded. She could hear everybody talking about the clasp. It was a tense time.

Mavis's voice, tart:

'No doubt she'll get another soon enough.'

And among the litter of paper, Mark:

'We ought to search everybody—line up the whole house-party, butler and all.'

Hearst was at H. J.'s side, still eager to be of service: 'Couldn't we organise it,' he said—'form a line of beaters from one side of the room to—' but tailed off as H. J. gave a great grunt of impatience.

And there was a general clink of shifted bottles and shushing of paper, and Monica saying all the time:

'I can't think *where*, I can't think *where*.'

Sandra suddenly saw that only she was doing nothing, simply staring goggle-eyed at nothing—the most obvious way of attracting attention! She jerked herself into action. But acting the pretence of searching, she became over-energetic—overturning in-trays into out-trays and vice versa, lifting up a heavy duplicator and thus revealing Mark's hidden Margaux, even squatting down to run her fingers round the men's trouser-cuffs.

Knowing the search to be useless, it seemed the more endless. Then it struck her that Monica had been into H. J.'s room to telephone Ralph's home. But didn't it solve everything? Couldn't she announce it before Monica remembered, so that everyone would hear? Then let Monica look around in there unsuccessfully? And later go in herself and wedge the clasp under something?

'Monica, weren't you in Mr Deane's room telephoning? Perhaps it's in Mr Deane's room?' she shouted in a radiant false voice.

Everyone looked up.

'Mr Deane's room!' Sandra said in a lower voice, pointing.

'I know the direction,' Monica said, looking at her with a new intelligence. Nevertheless, she went.

Jill whispered to her:

'Trouble ahead! I think H. J.'s ratting on taking her out tonight, too.'

'How *do* you know?' Sandra asked, in wonder at Jill's sharp ears. And Jill just winked one of her frank, blue, purple-circled eyes.

Then Quentin came out of his office holding a strong torch. 'This'll bring a twinkle from the stones themselves,' he said peering round enthusiastically.

'They'd better twink quick,' Mark said, staring suddenly pale-faced through the door to the passage, 'before we know what's hit us.'

Hearst and H. J. looked to where he was pointing.

'Oh God, no,' H. J. prayed, and the terrible tiredness sank its folds again over his face.

'Blimey!' Hearst said, as he saw what approached them in the corridor.

'No luck,' Monica was saying as she came out of the inner office. Sandra was opening the drawers of her desk one after the other, announcing in tones loud enough for most to hear:

'Just in case it slipped into one of my drawers. One of my drawers might have been the littlest bit open.'

Neither saw what the men were looking at.

Monica came straight over to her, and to the point:

'Or your bag? The littlest bit open too?'

Sandra's insides jumped with fright.

'Monica!' she breathed in a small voice, 'Monica, *really*!'

Mark was backing away from the corridor, an uneasy look in his eye.

'Why not a proper line-up?' he threw at Monica as he passed. 'Why don't we all strip?'

As on a theatrical cue, at the word 'strip', Sue Blair appeared in the doorway, brilliant and poised—before she was pushed into the room by a bottle-necked horde of laughing, singing, chattering bodies bringing forward endless fresh faces, fresh noise, fresh bottles waving.

Monica paled beneath her powder.

'The Pool!' she gasped.

Saved! Sandra wanted to embrace and kiss Sue with all her heart and lips.

'Yippee!' yelled the Pool. 'Yow!' they yelled.

Hearst, Mavis, H. J. and the others fell back nervously against the walls and files.

'Brudders n'transisters, praise d'Lordosis!' yelled a small girl called Shelagh Nussbaum, waving a radio set at them. A freckle-faced clerk leapt on a chair and megaphoned his hands like a radio-commentator: 'Well here we are folks at Foggy Bottom. It is a grand day. The President's in the pink—' but the rest was overcome as the transistor went on full blast and they all rushed at H. J. their boss.

In a second he was encircled by eager faces and bottles raised round his glass like the packed snouts of a multiple pom-pom.

'Down the hatch, Mr Deane!' shouted a Miss Maclure with a skittish leer.

'Avril!' gasped her friend Pam Currie, and apologetically to H. J.: 'We're making our round, see?' Relations with the executives were friendly and informal—but this was formal friendliness, a very different matter.

Sandra was automatically checking them: Pam Currie had cut off her hair, there was a young man with an Iroquois haircut and a face like a devil who always frightened her, and another pink-faced fellow she always thought rather sweet. Bossom had tagged on, with his own tag of Bone. It felt like a battalion—but there were not really more than a dozen of them—eight girls and a few clerks collected on the way.

A very tall book-keeper sat down at Ralph's desk and pretended to telephone a raw material order:

'Ten horns of Abyssinian civet by Tuesday, Mayhew, or there'll be a stink.'

It was an old joke. Those who knew about Ralph laughed uneasily. To cover it, Mark said once again:

'What about our line-up? We haven't found the clasp yet—'

And Mrs Tovey suddenly shouted: 'He says we're to have identity parade, I'm sure I don't know.' And accustomed as a cleaner to being suspected, she began to go about repeating this, as if to emphasise her personal innocence.

'Well, why not?' Mark said. 'Something to do?' and he went to follow Mrs Tovey.

The dresses of all these new girls whirled the room with sudden new colour. Everybody seemed to be talking at once again. It looked once more like a proper party, like the one Sandra had seen down below through the window. Couples had started a shuffling jive in one corner; they kept raising their hands in high loops, as if they were playing oranges-and-lemons.

Sandra saw Monica's back turned, quickly picked the clasp from her bag and palmed it to the neck of her dress. She dropped it in. She felt it catch in the centre of her brassière. She took a deep breath of relief. The pin dug into her. She hollowed her chest, sat there for a moment with her back hunched.

'Hello,' said Avril Maclure to Pam Currie across the room, 'what's up with that Sandra Lee?'

'That's the way the martini dries,' Pam said.

'Come on, everybody,' Mark said, walking about with his arms wide, 'all our new friends over that side—all the old guard under suspicion here . . . come on, line up Tiny, Mavis, Jill, Alec Quentin! And you, Mrs Tovey!'

'Ident'y parade,' sniffed Mrs Tovey. 'I told you so.'

H. J. was stretching his mouth into a game laugh—his whole square face howled like a Greek tragic mask.

'We're all in the same boat,' he said, giddy with democracy, linking arms with Jill.

'Is it a game?' cried different members of the Pool, as they were shepherded together opposite the suspects.

'This is Michael Grant,' said a new pipe-in-the-mouth voice from the transistor, 'bringing you *Studio Party* and here we all are, bright lights and fair ladies—it's all tremendous fun—there's Jimmy over there, and Mona and Tom and Hilda, and who's that, ye-e-es, Esther and Ron! And Don.'

He went reciting the Christian names, like a little book of Genesis, of people presumably known to worshipping listeners, while at the Allasol office party the twenty or so present were at last lined up opposite each other. Mark had become unusually vivacious and now went up and down the row of 'suspects' aping The Man from the Yard.

'When did you last see your father?' he asked Mrs Tovey, who shot back out of line startled, her cherries shaking. 'Who's baby are *you*?' he quested of the big bulk of Tiny Hearst.

Most were now laughing and acting up to this easy fooling. Some of the Pool giggled, others stared with wonder, others expressed simple boredom or disgust.

Only Monica was annoyed. She said to Mark:

'It's all very well playing about—but that clasp's worth something.'

H. J. tried with unconcern: 'She's right, of course, Mark—we ought to look seriously—'

'And I hope for your sake, Mrs Tovey finds it in the morning,' Monica snapped.

'I have *not* got it!' Mrs Tovey shouted at her. 'Come here for a quiet Christmas drink and find yourself in ident'y parade—'

Sandra was standing upright, leaning slightly back-wards. The pin, she thought desperately—as long as it hurts it's all right, it won't have slipped. For supposing, now she had to stand, the clasp fell through at her feet?

Mark was going along the line with a bottle and glasses: 'Truth Drug? Truth Drug?' he was saying.

Sandra tried to smile—but the joke was too near the knuckle, it could too easily turn serious: somebody goes too far, in a second the brightness sours. And the Pool was getting restive. It was no fun being shoved up against the files—and only to watch the thumping slow fun of these antic elders.

With one hand to her bosom to steady the pricking pin, she tossed back her drink. This was the drink that did it.

VIII

'HERE we go gathering NUTS IN MAY!' shouted the transistor.

'With Jimmy and Mona and Tom and Hilda and Ron and Don and Esther—' it shouted on, while Sandra leaned forward coughing, but still clutching her chest, and Bossom thumped her on the back dislodging the clasp, and she pressed harder, the pin dug itself further in, and she stumbled, not from this small pain but because now she was drunk.

'Here we go gathering Nuts in May!' yelled the Pool, joining hands, 'Nuts in May, Boing de Boing—' they sang.

Instinctively the line of suspects joined hands. And nobody saw Sandra slip back behind them and lurch to the glass partition leading to H. J.'s room. Carefully keeping an eye on Monica's back, she staggered through the opening in the glass and on into the inner office. She swung his door in a slam behind her—but even then caught it in time, closing it softly just as the Pool danced forward chanting Nuts-in-May and Mark's line stepped out joyfully to meet it.

H. J. suddenly forgot his troubles—he surged forward towards the Pool singing strongly, for Nuts-in-May was something he understood. Gone the awkwardness of talk, forgotten for a moment that damnable clasp and Monica's rising temper—this was the party spirit, parties should have games and Nuts-in-May was a great leveller. He began to enjoy himself almost as much as if he were singing 'For he's a jolly good fellow.'

Monica had butted in to the line next to him to take command—she had not forgotten his hint of driving to the country that night. All linked together in grey suits, H. J. and Hearst and Monica and Mark appeared to be in uniform, like a chorus line, and with their faces distinguished the more for this.

Mark repeated to himself that he really *must* escape: but again found himself amused, and the dancing movement itself was a welcome unconstraint. Jill threw herself forward with a fine swirl of pleats and fun, Alec Quentin tip-toed birdily like a dancing don, Mrs Tovey was a jelly of giggles and berries. The Pool—with the exception of two couples still quietly jiving by the Investments file— broke all constraint, romping and stamping with joy, only conceding to their youthful sophistication an occasional 'boing' instead of Nuts or May.

Mavis smiled a grey half-smile as she let herself be led by Hearst's kindness. And to Hearst's eye her simple subservience gave her a kind of beauty, like the radiance that shines from the face of a plain woman as she gives herself to her lover, a guardless long look of original innocence. Prancing his great bulk by her side, his heart gently warmed.

Standing alone in H. J.'s room, Sandra saw none of this. But the singing echoed through and she closed her eyes in the darkness. Unable to know how most of them outside were guying the game, she heard their voices as she as a child had listened at children's parties, hiding shyly outside the room, fearful of the open game, terrified to hear her own name called—and she hated them all, and longed for that other kind of party in the office-well below.

We'll have Mrs Tovey for Nuts in May
Nuts in May
Boing de Boing

yelled the glad voices of the Pool.

She put her hands over her ears, and this made the hidden clasp bite deeper and she remembered through the muzz of drink what she had come in here for. She reached down into her dress to pick out the clasp; fumbled, pushed it further down.

She bent double to get at it—and at the same time looked round the room. Her eyes had got used to the dark. And neon lights from across the street outside threw in a reddish, motionless light. She hobbled a few steps towards the window, and looked down.

It was a main street. Buses and cars and people streamed below: and all over the sides of the buildings red and violet and yellow lights blazed their excitant appeals. It was the first time she had looked from this window at night. The lights were as alive as the cabaret signs of a night town: a foreigner might have thought it a centre bright with gaiety. But she knew what it was, its very brightness emphasised the hollow nothingness, it was bright with death, it was disappointment advertised. She howled inside herself, straightened up, and the pin dug her sharply above the navel.

H. J.'s office was furnished softly. A gleam from the

polished wood desk and the furry pile of the carpet and the presence of a long settee all announced in the half-light a quiet luxury insulated from the lino life of type-writers outside. In a mirror on the wall, beside which hung a curved brush for H. J.'s hat, she saw herself shadowed and lit with ruddy touches of reflected neon: she saw the pile of her hair, and the light on a high cheekbone, and a slim-waisted figure new and mysterious. She glanced down at the desk—where the blow-up of Sue Blair's naked back accosted her sharply.

We'll have Avril Maclure-hure to take her away
Take her away
Take her away.

sang the executive leaders.

A number of things in Sandra's mind clicked. Sue Blair's back, Sue appearing on Mark's word 'strip', all those added girls from the Pool, all the sense of lost prestige and disappointment—and the immediate prick-ing of the pin.

A blaze of life rose in her and she laughed out loud, bitterly and hard:

'I'll show 'em,' she said alone to the room, 'I'll give 'em nuts in their May!' And she wrenched at the back of her dress where the zip was.

The zip slid down, and she began to squiggle the dress down over her thighs. Soon it fell in a heap sacking her ankles. She stepped out of it, heart beating with bad glad joy, muttering and giggling to herself: 'Sue's not the only pebble, I'll Sue her good and proper . . .' and reached in beneath her slip for the clasp, which was easy now to find;

then stood for a moment wondering where to put it.

Cunning behind the rich blur of alcohol—put it near where Monica had telephoned! She knelt down and wedged it where the carpet furred up high against the gleaming wooden wall of the desk. Done.

And now—here goes! Up with the slip over her head, off with it, careful the hair—and away, slap down wriggling silk all over Sue Blair's blow-up! She stood for a moment to see in the mirror—light catching bare shoulders, bare midriff, the points of a white brassière, a metal glint of suspenders. Backing her, reflected in the mirror too, the wide night-window—and behind her body a sharp bright sign, an orange word against the night and her cabaret body, GORLAND BROTHERS. She raised her arms to her hips and swayed to and fro in a show-girl way, and against the song still chorusing from the other room her delighted lips began to hum well-known words:

A pretty Girl
Is like a Melody,

as now she began to walk in short rhythmic steps, H. J.'s rich pile her stage, and reached with her fingers in a graceful gesture, all to music, to the back strap of her brassière.

She felt hilarious and utterly strong. Ideas, flashes came rocketing through her in a muddled, mixed, brilliant way, and at each one she bubbled laughter and felt more radiant.

Really, I'm doing it for Bun—it'll be Sarawak or nothing after this first and last appearance! Really—for

Allasol, to shake the party up, for H. J.'s sake! My good heavens, I'll give 'em nuts in May, I'll put May in their nuts she found herself giggling by mistake and broke into a bigger bubble of joy at this, and lurched, and the brassière strap clicked free and as it loosened on her shoulders she clutched it to her and thought: Really—for Ralph!

A spirit of sacrifice, cool and determined, infused her. She raised her small pointed chin above the world.

Let this be an emblem of sacrifice . . . and she let the brassière fall. As it fell, so the thought of Ralph fell away as colder air struck her breasts and she felt suddenly these intimacies bared in the unfamiliar room, and clutched them, and shivered, and then gave a loud snort of private laughter. 'Hup!' she cried.

In the other room the game of Nuts-in-May proceeded. A few of the Pool grew tired or found themselves superior to it, dwindling to the side to drink and jive. But the hard core of H. J. and Hearst and others bounced stronger and stronger in what was becoming an athletic enterprise, and was certainly good staff-relationship, the executive human and playful, and youth at its giddy clean fling.

What jollier than the sight of Mrs Tovey, with her tough muscle beneath silks and berries, tugging Avril Maclure on a handkerchief across the line?

On a cold and frosty MORNING

H. J. yelled at the top of his voice, his great manful face popping its eyeballs out from under the boxer's hairy brow and squaring his mouth so that pipe-yellowed lower teeth came into view. Romping belly-forward but extra-ordinarily light on his feet, he gave Monica's hand an unmeant muscular squeeze in the general effort. 'Ow!' she squealed, and frowned up at what looked both excitingly huge but also boyish and spankable.

'This won't get us anywhere,' she hissed.

'Not meant to,' he gasped, 'GO GATHERING NUTS—'

'The clasp you—'

'Shh,' he breathed down big, 'IN MAY. Mustn't let on. COLD AND FROSTY. Real look later. WHO SHALL WE—'

'Why did you say you were driving home?' she hissed to his face bouncing up and down. 'You said you'd be staying—'

'Shhh,' he shhhed, 'that's fixed, don't worry darling. HA HA HA HA HA!' he roared with laughter at her to cover up, and at the same time covered Tiny Hearst with the same laugh.

Hearst laughed back. So he wasn't for the high jump after all? Relief—but really, the old bastard was un-predictable this evening. Then he felt Monica squeeze his hand. Hello, hello!

But she had only squeezed the wrong hand, she was still looking at her big H. J. and now a knowing smile parted her lips, showing the big pink tongue rolled waiting inside.

'Go and have another look in the office,' she pleaded.

'Okay,' he said.

Bottles all bounced up and down on the desks and files as there was another thudding tug-of-war.

'Hooray,' they all yelled, as Bone pulled Quentin easily across the line.

Then Bone suddenly exploded in a great sneeze, as if all his oil of youth had at last chosen to empty itself. 'You got de catahhr,' roared Bossom, kneading an invisible guitar, 'so make wid de sniffle.'

'HERE WE GO GATHERING—' they all started up again.

'Please,' Monica pouted.

'Okay—after this one,' H. J. shouted joyfully, as once again the two lines started up, and he was romping his body towards Sue Blair so pleasantly opposite, and the bottles all began to bounce again, and a tray of papers crashed to the floor scattering unnoticed, and Mavis's sister's veil re-appeared for a moment wrapped round a big dusty down-at-heel mailing clerk's shoe.

Overwhelmed in his little box the mouselike mumble of Michael Grant went on gamefully giving the world a good time with Esther and Hilda and Tom and Tim . . . Ron and Don. And why, there's *Peter*. . . !

Sandra's neon-lit hands stayed covering her bare breasts, and her eyes went down to them, as if to see that they were really there—and then she flung her arms wide exposing herself to the mirror and the unwinking gaze of the Brothers Gorland outside in the fogging, frosting night.

She pirouetted, touched her nipples, arched her chest out to let neon light catch the upper curve of each breast; and stood still for some seconds, humming the last line,

Like a Mel-o-dy

The leather of H. J.'s chair shone dully, a pipe showed its dark knobbled wood against the mahogany desk-surround, the A.A. book winked across the room, a dark overcoat hung from a peg like a somebody waiting. She turned her body towards the overcoat; slowly raising her arms to make two white snakes above her head, she joined her hands flat like a dancer from the Orient, and gave her hips a long sway this way, that way.

'Ya-hooo!' she whispered to the overcoat. And thought, Should I go in like this? Or how shall I? Run in laughing, hair all muzzed, like a champagne-girl? Stride in with a smile, twisted, and raised eyebrows, *fatale*? Trip in, tiny steps, hands mincing in muff, head to one side—and all Allasol exploding with cries of 'Oh!' and loving laughter at such prettiness?

Truthfully winefully in the double-lens of drink, never seeing double but doubly strongly seeing one side only of a thought in question—she thought: No. Better the twisted smile or the downdrawn lips—for was this not most of all a sacrificial offering?

Sweet naked nymph to be immolated—yet chaired high at the same time? What shock, what amazement —but then what applause! The girls all envy of such good sportiness! Sporty yet sophisticated, *cosmopolitan*. And the men all throating together, like some deeply moved Russian choir, sounding her name in devoted unison, Sandra—Rah—Rah! Yet with all this she saw herself well fenced in, nobody would touch her.

She looked down her body and saw the long stockings and the flesh at the top but—then again darkness! The little black pants! She hesitated, her spinning head still treasured this last sanctuary—but then Nuts-in-May sang louder and she felt a sickening return of all her old fears and Ha! she said loud to herself and with the sense of relief of a woman losing her clothes at poker, with a wild joy simply to throw off her clothes anyhow, with the deeper wish of all women sometimes to play the bitch, she snapped down the elastic.

Quickly, efficiently, not lurching, she stepped out of them and threw these traitors into the waste-paper basket. Anyway, courage told her, her rubbery suspender-belt was a long one.

Freed, she took a waltzing turn or two on the carpet. Then suddenly stood still. She had heard them calling for Sue Blair. Her chin dropped. No one had called for her. Nobody wanted Sandra for Nuts-in-May. Nobody—and abruptly she felt forlorn and left out, standing alone in the dark with everybody else having fun beyond a dark door outlined with chinks of yellow light ... again like a child, hatefully shy and with a deep and welling wish not to be left out.

'Hup, Mamzel Lee!' she said aloud go herself. 'What are we waiting for?' And she stretched her arms wide to embrace the room, and began to walk towards the door.

Then she stopped, and thought slyly:

'Tug o'war. Wait till they start singing again. After which—*A pretty Girl*,' she began to sing in a deep and dedicated microphonic voice. Oh Daph, she thought, if you could see me now!

Outside, Sue Blair was chosen for Nuts-in-May and Jill Jenkins to take-her-away.

These two now took the handkerchief in hand and stood bracing their legs, Sue's slenderly skirted, and Jill's more stalwart calves fortressed in her big grey pleated kilt. They stood laughing into each other's laughing eyes. Nearly hidden behind this laughter lay a look of morose brooding, like that in a cat's eye at the sight of a bird.

They were all lining up behind, clutching waists, to tug and win. Mark was still there; he had forgotten to look at his watch—the severely painted, sixteen-year-old Shelagh Nussbaum from the Pool who had been dancing opposite him, had just shouted: 'S'you later, violater.' He was still mumbling to himself in ecstasy.

Hearst had his little fingers on Mrs Tovey's ample waist, on what felt through the silk like an ironclad's battleworks. Mavis had her hands on the jacket of her normal boss, Alec Quentin, who was studying with interest a raised mole on the back of Monica's neck, which itself was poking forward to whisper to H. J., whose arms embraced gingerly the skinny body of Bossom, who clutched Jill herself.

Monica whispered: 'Go now, while there's a chance. Go on!'

With Bossom in his hands, H. J. saw that if he had to go and look for the damned clasp, this was as good a moment as any. He disentangled himself and slipped away to his office.

Most of the Pool were forming a snake behind Sue

Blair and about balanced in strength, if not in weight, the sausage of executives.

Then it was One Two Three and—Pull!

And all pulled, and Sue's and Jill's feet stayed square, slipping an inch, recapturing it, and knuckles white round the handkerchief, which surely must itself burst in two beneath the stress. Tugged and tugged—faces grew redder, little tongues panted out, and what had started with laughter grew grimly serious.

Then the devil-faced young mailing-clerk detached himself from his jiving-partner and crept in a wide self-effacing circle round the filing cabinets towards Jill Jenkins, his hand holding something behind his back.

And H. J., breathing heavily after his romp, turned the handle of his office door and looked in.

The open door threw in light from the office, his hand that should have switched on the light was fumbling a handkerchief across his brow, and his mind was fumbling too.

He stood there staring straight at Sandra's dark naked figure frozen motionless by his desk, and lit here and there by the rosy glow from Gorland Brothers.

He stood wondering why he had come. Something had been driven right out of his mind. Why? It happened too much nowadays. And the breathing too, short of breath, middle-aged, past it . . . he shook his head as if to rid his eyes of something that should not be there, the wool of mounting years, as they continued their surveillance of Sandra's figure.

Sandra stood still as a statue, her heart pumping like a wild animal caged.

Man-figure in lighted doorway, man's eyes finding her . . . what do? where go? through ground?

Terror kept her so still that no hands clutched at her nakedness, no tremor of movement but the heart thudding and the lungs swelling with held breath, and terror that all this moving inside must play all over the skin of her seen body . . . a long exposure of slow-reeling seconds as she saw the figure to be H. J.'s, and that this was his private office in which she stood undressed, and wondered: Was he there alone or at the head of a crowd of others to come pouring in upon her? Though the light was still off, she felt all light around her already, the laughter from outside was loud and bright as eyes.

Then H. J. coughed—a muted cough as if to announce his presence—and lowered his head, turned away and left, closing the door quietly behind him.

Like a soft white moth in the half-light of Gorland's remote flame she seemed to shrivel, her poise all evaporated, and she sank shuddering down in the leather armchair at the desk. He had never said a word. Only the cough—the terribly recessive gentlemanly rebuke.

Thus at Allasol the taut blancmange of breasts, the dark areolae and the piled hairdress of what appeared in the reddish dark to be an Eastern princess took the executive chair.

But no one came to witness, the pale-skinned softness sat alone among dusky leathers, tobacco and heavy polished wood, and her shoulders crumpled, she hid her face and began to cry quietly to herself: 'Oh Lord, oh Lord in heaven what now? I can't, I can't.'

'Can't remember, can't dance a step but I'm winded,' sighed H. J.'s mind, 'I'm old. Beginning to like chrysanthemums too much too . . .' as he closed the door behind him, and faced the lighted outer office.

Yet something else, momentous but also not remembered, pulled at his mind. The dramatic device called a 'double-take', when the comedian does not at first see what he is looking at, and only seconds later jumps to realising it—this is based on truth. At such moments the mind truly prefers to sleep, rejecting what will upset it. Something like this had happened to H. J. as he looked for those acute seconds into his office. Disbelief is easier than new belief.

'I must play more golf,' he muttered as his hand slid off the doorknob. 'Pulpy kidney,' he thought.

Then, as he walked back to the party, his 'double-take' expanded into what is perhaps the longest ever recorded —for it never took at all.

All he felt was an overwhelming desire to see Sue Blair again. Possibly the unseen vision of a naked Sandra had reminded him of Sue Blair's photostat—but at the same time the whole office seemed to explode as that devil-faced young mail-clerk let off a fire-cracker exactly under Jill Jenkins's well-braced pleats.

Thunderflash! Yells! Powder-stench! Jill jumped as though raised on the hot air of the firework, her skirt forming a momentary slight parachute. As she came down she let go the handkerchief and was pulled smartly backwards in midflight by her collapsing comrades.

'Yow!' came screaming high. Shrieks from everyone, a typewriter crashed to the floor; and then droning displeasure: 'Shame!' 'Who was it?' 'Of all the rotten—'.

Many months later, perhaps, the image of Sandra would clarify—bringing sensations of madness, the feeling that he had seen something of which he had no real record. But now the explosion, the cries, the violent scattering of the Nuts-in-Mayers occluded everything. He was convinced that at last one of Quentin's retorts had blown. He rushed in, shouting:

'Good God! Good God! What's this?'

And propelled by his unremembered vision, he raced straight for Sue Blair, who lay, a tangle of brilliant legs, on the floor. Like a big bear he bandied out his arms and hugged her to her feet. At the same time he saw the typewriter on the ground and spoke sharply sideways to the mailing-clerk:

'You there! There are limits, for heaven's sake!' And added severely: 'After poor Mansford's lost his wife, too.'

Monica was tugging his arm away from Sue Blair's waist, where it seemed to have stuck. But at this mention of Mansford after several rounds of Nuts-in-May her eyebrows shot up really amazed at him.

'Did you find it?' she said.

The clasp! Of course! He let Sue go and said irritably:

'No. And really Monica, there's a time for everything. Now, with poor Mansford's trouble . . .'

He took out a cigarette to steady himself.

Monica looked at him with wonder.

'It's not true,' she sighed, 'it's not really true.'

'What's not? Pick up that typewriter, someone.'

As if to emphasise the need for order, he kicked up one leg like a big dog and neatly inserted the match from his cigarette into his trouser cuff.

Monica shrugged her shoulders:

'Might as well give up, I suppose, with this lot stamping on everything. Where's Sandra?'

'Sandra?' he said, in an oddly loud voice.

At the sound of a name Avril Maclure took it up, and sang out in a funeral key:

'We'll have Sandra Lee-ee for Nuts-in-May!'

And several others of the Pool, still smoothing themselves out, took it up like a dirge to put a derisive end to the game:

'We'll have Sandra Lee-ee . . .'

At the sound of her name Sandra sprang up with cat's quickness, clutched her brassière and snapped it on. In the next second she was shovelling the slip over her head, and then the dress. But tears still rolled down her cheeks, and she was shivering with cold and hurry.

She had sat collapsed in the chair for nearly a minute, loathing all the fear that came flooding in. And she had failed through no fault of her own, which made it somehow worse. She shrank only like someone caught without their clothes on, with a nightmare smallness. 'I *did* try, I *did* try,' she kept sobbing.

And she listened to her name, and the old childhood

terrors again returned, the breathless hiding in the echoing passage while pink-flushed voices laughed her name loud to go out on the floor alone to pull and—lose. She caught the derisive note, already mocking her. She tried to grit her teeth against her sobs, her mouth made a thin weak line of lipstick.

Over to the light-switch—and light crowded the room with abrupt new danger—the mirror, God the sight of her!—and no bag—quick—fingers dabbing all over face—how much had H. J. told them, was he the kind to tell? Or keep it sniggered up? What had that cough meant?

Her hands scurried up and down herself straightening and fixing, patting and smoothing a dozen things in as many seconds, and then she was hurrying to the door—but there stopped. For why hurry? To face the music? To get away from herself, to run away from herself inside herself as people panicked do?

Hand on doorknob, she stopped, and listened, for outside they too had stopped chanting her name ... they would all be standing with their eyes on the door waiting for her to come out.

Cold fear again, worse than ever. But this time it gave her new courage—it brought out the big old defence: 'Who the hell are they? Who do they think they are?' and she swung the door open with head held high.

No one at all was looking. Practically every back in the room was turned. Her heart jumped. Was it intentional, the big snub?

But no one even seemed to notice her come out

through the glass partition. As she passed Mavis, Mavis said cheerfully:

'I nearly jumped out of my skin, didn't you?'

'Skin?' she shuddered. 'Yes,' she said nervously, looking carefully round. Had no one even noticed her absence? No one knew?

But then H. J. himself bobbed up from almost underneath her. He had been bent down looking at the crashed typewriter. He was still thinking of it.

'No one seems to know where to stop,' he said, glaring at Sandra.

'I was too hot,' she lied, 'I had to slip something off,' she added and fled.

Monica looked at him curiously.

'Let something off?' H. J. said. 'It wasn't her, was it?'

'You know it wasn't. Or don't you? Where were you? Where was she?'

'Looking for the clasp,' he whispered, 'forget it.'

'I shall begin to think it *was* paste, soon.'

He flinched.

'Now, that's no way to talk'—he rolled lowered lids to right and left quickly, like a boy cheating—and added 'Darling' in a whisper.

Monica gave him the cool oriental whites of her eyelids:

'Anyway,' she said loudly, 'now you've been rescued from the rude clutches of Miss Blair—don't you think we might be getting on?'

'Look, Monica, I meant to say earlier—dinner yes, but I *must* drive home later.'

'Over my dead body. You've had too much—you'll lose your licence.'

'It's the family, Monnie, I've promised to put up the holly, they'll all be waiting . . . .'

'Christmas Eve'll do for that,' she said decisively.

'But we're all going out—the whole fam—'

'Come on,' she said loudly, 'we'd better leave. Remember last year. Merrydew and the L-M file?'

H. J. crumpled at the loud 'we'. What would she say next? He looked round at the disorder of the room.

'I don't know why I do it,' he said, 'I really don't.'

'Because it pays,' she snapped, taking his arm in full view of all.

Mark had wandered over:

'I'd better be going too,' he said, planting his feet firmly. 'Good Lord, look at Sandra! She's not going to be—'

They all turned to see Sandra who had gone to sit against the wall with Hearst. She was jolted forward, she sat as if kicked from within, her mouth open, a look of horror on her face. They held their breaths.

'A little of what you boing-dy?' giggled Jill coming up with a bottle of Yugoslavian Riesling. And Sandra slowly extended her glass, as in a dream. She had just remembered she had left her pants in H. J.'s waste-paper-basket.

IX

INTO Hearst's heart had come a feeling to protect and help Mavis. He recognised her loneliness—and his heart spoke, without knowing it, from its own alone-ness.

He had just suggested to Mavis that they go and have a little food together on the way home. He had made it sound as though he himself was desperately hungry—which was partly true. She would be helping him with her company. 'Roll-mops,' he had said, fluttering his sandy lashes. 'Hot sausages,' he had licked. 'Know a little bar.' She had agreed gratefully—adding a pre-emptive 'As long as we're not all night' to sharpen off a warm feeling she too felt.

'Then I'll go and tidy up,' she was saying, when Sandra had joined them in full flight from H. J. 'I shan't be two ticks,' Mavis said, and left them together.

Hearst was sitting behind a desk, Sandra squeezed on to a chair beside him, picked up a glass of yellowish stuff and drank it off. It was whisky. She coughed and laughed—laughed quite freely again for the first time. And now she found herself talking and talking to Hearst, spirits glibly rising again. While just then that transistor began to play, and all the Pool to hum the spine-tingling melody of the poundingly popular *Yours, Yours*.

Then she asked him point-blank whether he lived alone, and where, and how. Hearst wondered at this; but he was obsessed with certain common-sense innovations in his home-life and most ready to speak.

'The fridge and food *not* in the kitchen,' he had said emphatically as if preaching a new faith, 'but in the *sitting-room*, where they're to hand. And what if I told you I dressed for dinner every night? What about that? Pure sense—wear out the old dinner-jacket, never use it nowadays. Undress when you go out, black tie when you're in—that's the rule.'

She had nodded to this without surprise, informing him roundly that he was a great big man and so could do what he liked, whereas a girl—why, the things that happened to *girls*! And she had straightway embarked with silvery little laughs upon the story of the blonde-wigged man who had put on her dress, on that distant night which still affected her so.

Hearst listened amazed. As if to match the intimacy of such a story, she had leaned against him. So that he could not stop one of his hands settling on her thigh under the desk, and feeling the suspender buckle and the warmth there.

She seemed not to notice, she was all story. With his free hand he reached for a chocolate dragee, and crunched this slowly and richly between dentures which sank with blind savour into the brittle texture. He was astounded, and excitedly guilty, yet kept a breath-held ease, calm above all in case the fragile bubble should burst.

It had been in the middle of this story that Sandra suddenly felt a chill blow up her skirts—or was it simply a feeling of lightness there, of insecurity?—and remembered about the pants.

The Pool had just reached the final and climacteric line, after three rising 'yours,'

On-leee

which now they chanted long and harmonious.

Sandra jolted up, and at the same time her hand clutched Hearst's on her thigh. In her fright, she held it there tight. Heavens! she thought with the instant insecurity of a girl used to the feel of this slight armour. And then, Who'll see them? Was the waste-paper-basket well under the desk? How deep? What laundry marks? Mummy sent them once! She was quite certain that they would be recognised as hers.

She looked over at the vestibule door. No chance to get back. H. J. and Monica were standing there, whispering.

Hearst sat tense with pleasure and guilt, only the bulge in his cheek moving up and down, as if something separate and alive were inside. But suddenly she removed her hand from his. That was when Jill came up with her bottle:

'A little of what you boing-dy?' Then she looked round and sniffed: 'Hello, who's using Moujik?'

'I'm ready,' said Mavis, from the door.

Hearst seemed to wake up from the fat sleep of a big cat.

'Oh—um—are you? Good,' he said with falling face.

He got up to go, putting on for Mavis a stiff smile. His warmth for her had been quite overcome by another.

Yours, Yours.

sang Sandra to the room at large, hardly noticing this departure.

I'm yours,

she sang. She had suddenly recovered, she suddenly saw

206

how she was a knickerless woman with a glass in her hand, dangerous and free!

'You won't be anyone's at this rate,' Jill said, 'will she, Mrs Tovey?'

'I've just seen yellow stuff,' said Mrs Tovey, 'all over them hyacinths. I've only got one pair of hands.'

'Oh lord, Mrs Tovey!' Sandra said, suddenly remembering Ralph Mansford's carton, and his last words. 'Mrs Tovey, you're the only way out.'

'If they expect me,' said Mrs Tovey, 'to go down on my hands and knees up all these ruddy dead flowers—with all else I've got, God knows what under m'six-legger, but yours is the grey contemp'ry, isn't it, dear? I love your album.'

'You've looked into my book?'

She smiled—she saw that it might be Mrs Tovey who would finally find her pants.

'If there's one thing I can't resist,' said Mrs Tovey, helping herself to a drop of Riesling, 'it's a photo-album. I just love snaps. Though yours is different, artistic I'd call it. Isn't Don Terry a love?'

It was like a personal compliment.

'Ever so wonderful,' Sandra said, warming to this genial new ally.

Then she decided to take the plunge, and whispered to Mrs Tovey all about the carton.

The geniality faded, grimness narrowed Mrs Tovey's pin-bright eyes. But not from distaste. She had the distant look of a sea-captain lost in far horizons. It was technical interest.

'Smashed glass *and* sick,' she said. 'It's a facer.'

'Whatever *are* you two talking about?' said Jill.

'Too heavy to move,' Mrs Tovey said to herself, 'and full of good bottles underneath. Hm.'

'Still,' she said brightly to Sandra, 'if it's all done up neat, it'll keep. Cheerio, goodlooking!'

This last to Mark, who was dawdling very slowly past them towards the door.

'I was just running along,' he said.

Jill said: 'Do ask them what they're talking about. It's all Greek to me.'

Mark put a resigned look across his face.

'Don't ask me to ask nothing,' he said. 'I'm past it. Observe my Grande Poolette over there!'

He pointed to where Shelagh Nussbaum was standing jigging to the transistor's rhythm. Two thick strands of her straight hair curved round like scimitars to meet the corners of her mouth—now she had the ends of both tresses gripped in her little teeth and was sucking away with a kind of ferocious concentration as she watched the movements of her feet.

'Must have washed it in beer,' Mark said. 'But Sandra, my poker-face, *you'd* appreciate this—she just referred to the venerable H. J. and myself as "You and your uncle, Oedipus-Schmoedipus." And who knows but she isn't right?'

Sandra laughed wildly—because she wanted to, not because she had understood.

'She intends to spend her summer vacation,' Mark added 'in a place called Jugoslavia-I-go-nuts. With a couple of Cats and Chicks. She's Ape about Abroad, she said. And this, mind you, is the same lady who daily, on behalf of the Mission, types out long letters about rare esters, about methyl heptenone, colloid mills and even foot-operated tube-crimpers. Can *you* tell me how she reconciles these two assumably separate worlds?'

'But Mrs Tovey!' Sandra suddenly said, 'the trouble is it won't keep!'

'The chick's a genius,' Mark said, 'a real broiler.'

Over by the electric clock, with its long red finger dispensing private and ceaseless magic, the chick-genius was gesturing a black-lacquered nail towards H. J. and Monica, and then to Sandra's group.

'The poppas and mommas ain't playing no more games. Clicks they're making,' she said to Avril Maclure.

'Come again?' asked Avril.

'Get fell in, the whistle's went. Let us git, Mrs Pitt.'

'Lead the way, Mrs Hay,' said Miss Maclure, picking up the transistor.

And quite suddenly, in a flock, like a band of strolling players, the Pool left.

They went playing and singing, and as one body—a most efficient migration. And in the office so suddenly bared, Sandra took a quick look over at Monica and H. J. They were still whispering. But at that moment Monica looked over at Sandra.

'I'd quite forgotten about Sandy-Marge,' she said, 'she looks happy enough—the cat swallowed the canary, clasp and all.'

The strains of *Yours, Yours* fading along the passage

abruptly changed to wild cries of greeting and laughter. They both turned to look.

'Oh God,' H. J. swore, 'Olle Olsson!'

A very tall man stood in the doorwary. He wore a freshly pressed blue suit. He was shining with freshness, and stood with his heels pressed together.

Monica said: 'The Stockholm agency? But you weren't expecting—'

'He ought to be on the Isle of Wight.'

Jill clutched Sandra's arm. Her mouth fell open, her eyes clouded over.

'Lor, what a smasher,' she breathed.

Sandra rose to her feet and went to the door without a trace of shyness.

'Can I do you for anything, sir?' she said.

'Olsson,' he said. 'You are having a party,' he informed her, bowing and smiling broadly across his whole long handsome rock-grey face.

Her eyelids fluttered, she put a hand on one hip, gave a little nudge to her torso.

'How did you guess?'

H. J. was crossing the room with arms outstretched.

'Olle! Olle! I'd no idea, this is a grand surprise!' he shouted.

Mr Olsson bowed again and smiled from his great height:

'I'm a bore crashing in so!' he said in perfect English. 'My plane was late, I have a night to stay in London. So. But I never knew your strong silent English offices were so gay.'

'Staying the night?' H. J. laughed, seeing his chance. 'Then we must have a talk! What are you doing for din—'

Monica cooed quickly: 'Mr Deane's staying in London too. You'll be able to meet for an hour tomorrow morning!'

Mr Olsson's body swayed like a slender blue tree in the wind:

'Great! But there's nothing that won't keep till after Christmas. You're engaged tonight?'

'What a shame, yes,' said Monica. 'Of course, he wasn't expecting—'

H. J. mumbled: 'At least, we've a chance of a drink now! How are the Male Toiletries doing?'

He handed Mr Olsson a dirty glass of whisky.

'Vintage does very well,' Olsson said, leaning backwards not to appear to look too closely at the glass, 'but Worsted's slow. *Skål!*' he added bravely, tossing off the spirit—and then looking H. J. hard in the eye in the traditional manner.

At this suddenly severe gaze H. J. felt that Olle was being rather hard on him about Worsted. He turned to Mark and said:

'I always knew that damned name was wrong. Worsted indeed. You get the best from worsted—ridiculous.'

'But these are Swedish sales. In Swedish,' Mark said evenly, 'to Swedes.'

Alec Quentin breezed up in his overcoat.

'Now, now mustn't talk shop!' he said. 'How are you, Olle? You find us celebrating.'

Olsson bowed again.

Mark laughed:

'Alec, why don't you fixate this Viking with a really stiff one from the lab—Gurgun Balsam oil, ginger-grass, dash of benzaldehyde—'

Quentin's eyes sparkled:

'Just the job!' he said. 'And a drop of turps to make his wee-wee smell of violets.'

He coughed, noticing the ladies.

'Oui, oui, as the French say,' he apologised to Monica, 'it's a scientific fact. Turpentine affects the uric—'

Mark yelled:

'Eureka! Alexander the Great's you-know-what smelled of violets—it was the resin wine!'

Olsson was smiling to and fro:

'I thought I spoke English,' he said, 'but I don't understand a word—'

'Mr 'Olly,' Jill said, '*I* haven't understood a thing for *hours*.'

'Ha ha ha,' laughed Olsson, 'that's a good one.'

'Oh, Mr 'Olly, what a lovely Christmassy name you have—' Jill began, but H. J. took Olsson by the arm, and turned him away. 'About that Worsted, Olle—'

'It was a good sell in,' Olsson said, immediately grave, 'but the printer was slow on point-of-sales material.' And then, speaking in the calm tones of a male nurse, he outlined to H. J. and Monica the troubles of *Worsted*.

'He's a foreigner, isn't he?' Jill whispered to Sandra. 'But he looks sort of English, doesn't he? And he speaks so well. Actually, it's funny.'

Both girls and Mrs Tovey watched him appreciatively, whispering. Like most Swedes he looked English in a way that most Englishmen would like to look, with his great stature, and his long and violently handsome face, his extra clean appearance, and a kindly laughing gravity. Yet he was foreigner! So he probably had hidden in him the passions of the Latin south, where foreigners are supposed to come from. Indeed, a few elegancies of gesture betrayed him. Had he come to save the situation? they thought. For now the Pool had left, the party looked empty or over—yet it was still mid-rush-hour.

'Well,' said Mark to Sandra, 'one for the road?'

Sandra held her glass out again.

'Skol!' she giggled.

And for the first time the room took a tilt, and began very slowly, as if seen from a Ferris wheel, to go round. She gripped her jaw, frowned, and stopped it: laughed, and started it again.

'What's up?' said Jill. 'Oh, isn't he wonderful.'

'Everything's up!' Sandra laughed, throwing her arm up rather wildly, 'everything, everything! The curtain, the balloon, the game, the—SKOL!' she finished, as Olsson turned towards them again.

Mrs Tovey watched Sandra take a few short steps, hips swinging, towards Olsson, to stand blocking his way looking up at him and repeating, 'Skol!'

'Look at 'er!' Mrs Tovey said.

Olsson was used to it, it was a recognised joke with the English.

'Ah, you speak Swedish,' he laughed.

The huge figure above her swung like a handsome pendulum.

'What a funny name, Olle,' Sandra giggled, pronouncing it 'Ollay' as all the office did.

'It's no joke in Spain,' said the pendulum, 'when they're dancing.'

He sighed and straightened his bow tie:

'You get a crick in your neck, looking for all your new friends.'

'Well we're all your friends here,' said Sandra, linking an arm in his, 'whatever you may think,' and steered him a little away. She raised her lips and lowered her eye-lids: 'Now what are you doing all alone in the Big City?'

'Going to the Isle of Wight,' said Mr Olsson.

Sandra was undismayed:

'And if someone steals you before you get there?'

'Ha ha ha,' laughed Olsson.

She pushed out her underlip in a fetching way.

'You never know,' she said hoarsely, frowning to keep the pendulum still, and at the same time managing to say to herself 'cheese' to make a photographic smile. Olsson watched this uneasily, coughed, and looked down at his drink.

'This is a marvellous party,' he said, 'how long is it going on for?'

Sandra shouted:

'Fini! But the evening's just begun!'

Her heart was now racing hard. A foreigner, a real foreigner! Everything suddenly seemed to be solved. Bun, Nevile were forgotten—she looked flushed and radiant.

Olsson bent down upon her his large and kindly smile, saying:

'And what are *you* doing for the evening?'

There it was! Now—play hard to get? Play into his arms?

'You look so very happy,' he said.

Sandra stiffened.

'Happy?' she said. She was just beginning to make her mouth droop into an interesting shape, tormented, mysterious, when Olsson leaned close and said:

'Tell me, what is the name of that girl over there?'

The shape of her mouth became even more interesting.

'Jill,' she snapped. 'Her name's Jill Jenkins.'

'Be a sport, and introduce me.'

'Certainly,' Sandra said. 'Oh yes, certainly, oh certainly.'

Jill was perched on a desk, swinging her legs, whirling her pearls round hard with one hand, her eyes still clouded and her face flushed, sultry, seductive, extraordinary. Sandra caught at her breath. She introduced them formally.

'Mr 'Olly,' Jill said simply, but gazing up at him with the clear approval which a busy man can value as half-the-battle won.

Within a minute, in front of Sandra, Mr Olsson had asked her out to dine and dance.

'Oh, but I couldn't,' Jill breathed, looking up into his eyes, her whole being now flushed with a kind of hot female musk, 'I've got to do the decorations.'

'Can't they wait?' said Olsson very gravely. 'Please,' he said.

'Oh,' Jill said. Then: 'I suppose I've got the day.'

'Of course,' said Olsson with a shade of wonder, 'you've got the day.'

'Then I will,' Jill's lips laughed, her pink healthy face and this new muskiness giving her the traditional glow of a hay-maddened milk-maiden.

'Excuse us,' Olsson smiled to Sandra, as to an old friend.

Then Sandra contrived a fearful gesture to hide her feelings, she clapped her hands, raised her right arm above her head like a snake, cried out

olé all!

and turned a complete circle.

Everyone looked round in surprise. Olle smiled nervously and said to her:

'*And*, of course, we would be delighted if you could accompany us, Miss er-er.'

Sandra raised her mask to him, and, though the room was buzzing and seemed to wish to turn upside down, spoke without a tremor.

'I'm sorry, but I have a previous date.'

'Ha ha ha,' laughed Olsson in large relief, 'I always knew you had. With your fiancé, lucky man,' he added swiftly glancing at her ring.

Sandra made a disdainful droop of her lips. That damned ring.

'Actually,' she said, for Jill, 'it's with a Mr Nevile Wrasse.'

But Jill only smiled very sweetly at this momentous confirmation of evil.

In many ways, this was the worst desertion, her woman's confidante gone. Alone now, she believed what she had just said. She shivered as she saw a piece of tissue paper billow up and fall in the heat of a radiator, as if it were alive. 'Oh Bun, oh darling Bun,' she cried silently, 'what have I done to you?'

Monica was pumping Olsson's hand:

'I've simply got to get this man off now, Mr Olsson, I *do* apologise.

H. J. was behind her, mumbling: 'Ring you early tomorrow, Olle—must rush. But you're in good hands, I see. Miss Lee's a rare one. And Alec'll look after you, where's Alec—oh! . . .'

But Quentin was already at the door in his tweed overcoat. 'Must be off,' he apologised eagerly. 'We live in the north, you know,' he added.

'Me too,' said Olle Olsson.

There was a last brittle laugh, a fumbling and buttoning of coats and the two directors and Monica went out through the door.

Monica turned at the last moment and stared at Sandra.

'I found the clasp in the inner office,' she said. 'It was by the waste-paper basket.'

No note of apology in her voice. It seemed to carry some extra meaning. Sandra stared after her speechless.

Then Olle and Jill suddenly left. Olle bowed to her, but Jill just drifted to the door in a kind of dream. Sandra watched Olsson's fine tall back, his smooth blue suit, his agile fresh foreigner's strength pausing with what seemed a most intimate deference to let Jill pass, before he too was gone, never looking back.

Desperately she swung round on Mark.

'Mark,' she said, 'have another—'

But Mark was looking with horror at the empty room.

'I really *must* go,' he gasped.

And he went.

She was left all alone with Mrs Tovey.

'Well, ducks,' Mrs Tovey said, nodding at the room, 'I can see I'll have to look lively tomorrow. Now what was your little trouble again?'

The room was flickering, wheeling, tilting, Sandra shook her head at the buzzing inside her head.

'My troubles?' she asked, looking closely at Mrs Tovey's bright round face. 'We'd be here a year.'

'The trouble what I said would keep,' Mrs Tovey said.

'Oh *that*! That's—' and at that moment a smell of Moujik came wafting all around.

'Mavis?' she said, turning.

But no one was there. Only Slaughter, the cat that lived down among the boilers and sometimes favoured the Allasol offices, now padded in slowly and possessively, sure as a lion, on heavy muscular paws.

Sandra sniffed;

'It's definitely Moujik where the broken bottles are,' she said.

'Oh, *Tibbs*!' shrieked Mrs Tovey. 'You *haven't*!'

Slaughter sat down in the middle of the room, raised a leg stiff as a crane, and with inward-thinking eyes lapped at himself. This little action, industrious and moving, showed up more than ever the sudden quietness of the room around.

'Oh Lord, Tibbs, if you have, you'll have glass in your tum!'

Mrs Tovey swung round bouncing berries at Sandra: 'Come on, we'd better see if he's been at it. Where is it?'

Again a long wisp of tissue rose from the floor and subsided like a little white ghost. From his sitting position Slaughter jumped a clear foot into the air and landed foursquare on his paws with arched back. He had been caught in mid-lick. Now a pink pellet of tongue stayed stuck out of his mouth like Turkish Delight. A chocolate-box lion, he began to stalk the wisp of tissue, which still breathed alive in the floor-draught.

'Looks full of life to me,' Sandra said quietly.

Usually she would have laughed at Slaughter's extraordinary movements—belly-crouch, lashing tail, head pecking from side to side, and the great leap through the air to land triumphant on the papery prey. It was Sandra who begged saucers of milk for this cat throughout the year, she loved it and mothered it with catnip-mice and once a rubber bone. But now she felt nothing. Only a sour feeling of failure in everything. A hot alcoholic weariness; full but empty. But the emptiness sourly called to be filled. Life must be got on with. Better go and get to that waste-paper basket. No, better first to divert Mrs Tovey—so she took her along to the little room where the carton was. At least she'd get that done for Ralph, she could get that done.

The flaps on the carton were still closed. Slaughter must simply have sat on the top. Mrs Tovey, in all her summery coloured silks, her mauves and berries, knelt down with an expert sigh, opened the flaps, and said:

'Hm! Handy.'

The smell of Moujik rose heavier than ever. The cartoned walls marked *Fragile* closed them round. What Sandra saw was narrowed to Mrs Tovey's kneeling figure and Ralph's carton, a set-piece all the brighter for the wine-darkness framing her eyes.

'Mrs Tovey,' she suddenly said, 'did you see my boy tonight? Were you here when he came?'

'Hm,' said Mrs Tovey to the carton.

'No, it was earlier. He's so tall, Mrs Tee, and kind of— well, kind-looking. He's strong, too. We'll be married soon. I'm going away, away abroad with him.'

'Straight?' Mrs Tovey said. 'Good luck to you. Now the first thing is, it's too heavy to shift. So whatever we do, we do here.'

'We've known each other years. It's always been Bun and me, really.'

'You've got your two rows of bottles broken on top, and your eight layers of good bottles packed under. So we can't tip it over. That's flat.'

'You feel you can trust Bun, he's a man you can rely on. Isn't it funny the way they're like that—great big things you can lean on, yet babies too?' Her heart was yearning deeply for him. She could suddenly cry, it hurt so.

'We have to start from the top. Item No. 1, you can't

put your hands in the glass and mess. Item No. 2 I'd cut holes in the bottom and swill my water through it if we had a sink handy. But we haven't.'

'I love him dearly,' Sandra sighed. 'He's got ways— oh, I don't know. Are you happy, Mrs Tovey?'

'The fire stinguisher,' Mrs Tovey said quietly.

'Are you?'

'Am I what?'

'Happy. With Mr Tovey, I mean.'

'I've got Mr Tovey at home all the time, you know.'

She seemed to think far away for a moment, her eyes looked down at the lace on her sleeve.

'Yes,' she said, 'I'm very happy. No, no good, it's a foam stinguisher, all foamy.'

'At home all the time?' Sandra asked.

'Make more mess than it's worth. Mr Tovey's in a chair, you know.'

'Oh—I'm sorry.'

'There's no need really dear. I've got him with me, haven't I?'

'Is it—was it—what?'

'Rheumatics. That bad. It might come to any of us. Though it was the camping did for Tovey, he had his Scouts you know. But we must be thankful for small mercies, he was getting to be a very violent man, they change. Now if only I 'ad—had my pair of rubber gloves . . .'

Sandra took a breath: 'Mrs Tovey, may I ask you something? Did you ever—were you ever—I mean, before Mr Tovey, did you ever have a boy?'

'undreds.'

'But did you, I mean—did you—?'

'What you getting at, miss?'

'I'm sorry, I shouldn't 've—'

'That's enough, then. And if you'll take *my* advice,' Mrs Tovey said, straightening up on her knees and looking at Sandra closely, her little blue pin eyes hard with a kind of contempt, 'you'll marry your man quick, if you got them ideas come to you.'

Sandra said weakly: 'I know, but it's different now to when you were a girl. Things are sort of—oh, people get about more—'

'Get it screwed on!' Mrs Tovey flared. 'We was young women weren't we, same as you? We had our feelings, and we didn't have no wings. My fambly, we slept eight in our room, you can't hide much that way, it was like a bloody farmyard nights. Still I kept myself to myself. If you want to keep yourself decent, you do, and that's all there is to it.'

'You don't understand,' Sandra said loud.

'Oh I don't, don't I?'

'It's just—I feel, when I marry Bun, is that *all*? I mean, is that all my life?'

Mrs Tovey suddenly smiled, put out her hand and stroked Sandra's cheek.

'There now,' she said. 'There's lots more'll come to you than you think.'

Sandra wanted to smile, but instead felt the old simple resentment at being told what to do. It would have been the same if her own mother had told her to do exactly the opposite, if in her up-to-date way she had told Sandra to go out and find some fun. The telling was the thing, whichever way it went. She wanted to decide for herself. Advice was only for airing a problem and confirming her own decisions.

'And if we take the plunge,' said Mrs Tovey returning to the mess of bottles, 'we're going to stink to high heaven. You'd smell like a 'arlot after this lot, and I've got more of my gentlemen to see—go on, dear, you go to him!'

'I can't. He's being syringed.'

Mrs Tovey gave her a dark look.

'You poor girl, they're all beasts,' she said.

'For his tropical inoculations. At the hospital. We're off to Sarawak, you see.'

'I don't know about that, I'm sure,' Mrs Tovey said of Sarawak, 'but it's a relief that man's not caught something. Be thankful for small. Haven't they got a waiting room? You could look at some nice books while they was finishing him.'

Sandra flung her arms round Mrs Tovey.

'You've hit it! Why did I never think? That's just what I'll do!' She had in fact thought of it: this was the affirmative push.

'All right,' said Mrs Tovey, 'but I haven't hit *this*, have I? If I got a cloth and took the top off, there's more will have gone down where the good bottles is below, it's all chinks. No,' she said with a big sigh, 'we'll have to get the whole lot out and wipe each one over. And be here till midnight, not me. Let sleeping dogs lie,' she said, closing the lid and groaning up off her knees. 'Poof! Keep me off the Dilly, I'd get copped.'

'Why, I remember where it is too, the name of the street!' Sandra said, and she pulled Mrs Tovey to the door. 'My bag's in the office,' she said, and they went back to where the empty room stared with all lights blazing and no one there. It was like a room found in the middle of the night, like a feast abandoned in calamity. Slaughter was fast asleep in one of Hearst's out-baskets.

'Let's have a wet,' Mrs Tovey said, and they both took a last glass from those bottles.

But now Sandra hesitated before drinking. The room had stopped its swaying. It was the moment to keep a grip on her head, and go sober to Bun.

But there was Slaughter opening one eye watchful, and Mrs Tovey jangling all her berries as she raised a filthy glass to the light to view the clarity of her wine, and giving a rumbling giggle—how, a moment before, could she so have resented this dear good woman?—and the room in such disarray, and in her mouth a clotted feeling that asked for more. So she took more. It shivered spirit down her spine. So she drank off another on top of it.

Mrs Tovey was casting a severe eye round the room:

'Who's going to turn off the lights, I'd like to know? Not that Bletch by the look of him. And are we locked up?'

She went towards H. J.'s door. Sandra's heart flinched. She had quite forgotten! But Mrs Tovey only pulled at the handle.

'*That's* all right,' she said, and chatted on, 'they must

have their yales, oh yes, the big babies, which a kiddertwo could open with his little finger.'

That's done it, Sandra thought. Yet would Bletch have a key downstairs? 'Come on,' she said, 'let's leave the morgue for the hospital.'

Mrs Tovey gave a little whoop.

'It'll be vice versa,' she cried, 'before this night's done.'

As they passed along the passage, they found Bossom all alone washing the Advocaat off the hyacinths with a pail of water.

'And they say miracles never,' said Mrs Tovey.

He jumped at the words and turned showing them a black eye, and his long lip bleeding.

'Oh, Bossom!' said Sandra.

His lip made a painful waggish monkey-stretch:

'Walking out with a lamp-post,' he tried, but half his spirit gone. 'Lord, how that post could kiss!'

Mrs Tovey began to say about putting cold meat on it, and the reception desk began, very slowly, to go round—Sandra said, 'Oh, poor Bossom,' and dragged Mrs Tovey on.

Out on the stairs a dark buzzing in her head made everything more shadowed, the hard iron trellis of the lift, the bare walls chocolate and cream, the broad Victorian stone steps. Clatter of high heels, soft thud of Mrs Tovey's plastic bootees, down and round and down.

What a party, she thought drearily—hell, it's been a fine party, in my new dress I kissed Ralph Mansford, and at a time like that, and I got Mark going, you could feel his excitement, and in my new dress given me by Nevile I stole diamonds from Monica and then I took my new dress off and stood revealed for all to see. . . .

'Poor man, and before Christmas too,' Mrs Tovey was going on about Ralph. 'Buried on Boxing Day, I wouldn't be surprised. . .'

Who was Ralph, she thought suddenly, that I kissed

'. . . I never had none all those years, try as we did, and that's why Mr Tovey went to his Scouts I hope.'

The voice going on reminded her, '*They must have their yales, the babies*' . . . O God, I'll have to go back and get them, she'll find them in the morning and she'll know they're mine, those laundry marks, she'll think: There's a fine one talking about the boy she's going to marry. . . .

'Mrs Tovey!' she cried out, 'who's got the keys to Mr Deane's room? How do you get in there on your mornings?'

'. . . the poor mite, will his sister look after it did they say? Bletch'll have them in his dug-out. But you can't be going all the way back there now?'

'Will Bletch let me?'

'I dare say. If I say.'

'And there's Mummy's transistor too!'

'Mummy's who? Well you won't get me up them stairs again with you, miss. Isn't it time to go home sweet home?'

X

HOME sweet home.

Hearst and Mavis had risen from the little saloon bar, tiled like a dairy, where up on hard stools they had eaten hot sausages and eels and watched each other in the mirror behind the bottles opposite. Together they had talked amiably but dully. And now, as soon as was decent, rose. Hearst had been quite upset by Sandra, and Mavis was not unwilling, for she had now regained all her composure, and really wanted the quiet of her room. This big man sitting next to her, with bulging suit and his cropped hair, was really miles away. He always had been. The jokes about the two of them in the office had been pleasantries, no more. She looked down at his little white fingers playing with a pellet of bread, and thought sadly: 'Nothing. Nothing.'

And then sighed, her spirits up again: 'Never mind, it's as better not.'

They went to the Underground together, and in the milling crowds, parcel-hung and some tipsy, parted, she for her room in Belsize Park, he for his Kensington flat.

And Mansford had left the hospital, two faces in mind, the raw red nut squalling among others in a line of white cots; and the pale vellum effigy of his own girl, grinning, in no sense reposed, like nothing he had ever touched, his wife and love and life, his Tilly.

With his sister he took a taxi all the way out to her

rockery-bound little house in Norbury. When they got there his sister's husband tactfully withdrew, but there was a ceaseless pounding of feet from the twins on the ceiling of the sitting-room. The electric logs wheeled their monotonous red flame. Nothing else in the room moved. The room was decorated for Christmas: but it was also cleaned and tidied, dusted and polished. The holly, the paper-chains, the coloured tinsel balls on the Christmas tree all hung terribly still. It looked less a room than a temple staged for pagan sacrifice. Over everything there dripped a dry lametta of silence, punctuated by the slow beginnings and sighing voice of his sister invoking a memory or a consolation, which only emphasised the warm, clean, dead quiet.

His throat rasped for another drink, but he would not take one; he wanted above all a clear mind. Occasionally he shivered even in the warmth of the fire, shuddering to be away but knowing his own home would be too quiet; and that all public places with their people would be as bad, and that finally he must stay here where there could be discussed all that follows death, registration, the funeral, the price of the coffin. And with these the one lively matter, the future of the child, usurper of love and hate.

While above all this his real mind hammered: Why, why, why? Why, if there is a God, why?

And: Why to me?

Alec Quentin sat at the wheel of his Hispano home-tuned with bits of Alvis and Bentley and even De Dion

Bouton, and purred loudly towards his big red house in a northern suburb. Slate roofed and with liver-painted eaves, it stood in a weedy firbound garden. Dark blinds hung askew in gloomy windows. None of the Quentins cared for appearances.

Twenty-year-old John Quentin was usually under a car or inside a wireless, when he was not at his job measuring wind pressures. Mrs Quentin had mixed interests—she bred broiling turkeys and fought for Prison Reform—and had little time for the vanities. The house was littered with the components of these mixed energies: a turkey-basket weighting the Holloway correspondence, a container of $C_{13}H_{20}O$ alongside a mixed stack of *Fur and Feather* and the *Motorcar*. Only Sukie, their seventeen-year-old daughter, was different: she swayed about the house painted like a spongy little doll and dressed in high teen-age fashion. She worked in a shoe-shop and coined the money. However, she was seldom at home, which was hardly the place for a young girl.

Towards these littered rooms and tattered sofas Alec Quentin drove. Should his family be there to greet him, well and good; should they not be there, equally well and good. He was proud of his family, and loved them. But he did not dwell on these matters. Bound up in his science, he was free. Life was not to be wasted in living.

Down and down went Sandra and Mrs Tovey.

At last the grand mahogany of the entrance hall, and Mrs Tovey said:

'Wait here while I winkle out old Bletch.'

Sandra wandered away past the empty lift-shaft to where it was darker by the basement stairs. From this gloom the pale figure of Bone appeared, zipping his flies. He whipped his hands away, leaving the little steel tab winking out.

'I socked him!' he cried proud.

'What, Bone? Who?' she said surprised.

'Bossom upstairs.'

'Bone!'

He eased his shoulders. His youthful oil glowed pallid in the gloom.

'It came over me sudden,' he said. 'Bossom made me pour that stuff on the flowers, and when he says after, get a bucket and clean it off Bone I says sudden clean it off yourself and he laughs and I say who are you laughing at take that laugh off your mug or I'll take it off for you and I did, suddenlike, it just come over me, I must've wanted to do it all the time, who's he think he is? Get a bucket, Bossom, I said. You should've seen.'

'I did,' Sandra said.

'Well then!' Bone said, a man.

From the lift Mrs Tovey called:

'He says will you come for the keys here?'

'I think you're a big bully,' Sandra said.

'Me?' said Bone astounded. His mouth fell right open.

She stared him straight in the eyes, through the gloom, and the stone stairwell echoed words taken from a film about delinquent youth, but odd from her lips.

'Why do you want to upset everything?' Sandra

intoned. 'Isn't there enough trouble in the world?'

She turned on her heel and chin-in-air left the boy unmanned. Tears of injustice rising, he whispered:

'Me bully Boss? Me bully *him*?'

Bletch was inside his hole where, through a curtain of rum and a blue haze of shag, he sat severely seeing double. At that moment he was addressing two Mrs Toveys, who stood in alarming summery colours, like ladies about to open fêtes, in his doorway.

Bletch's job was discipline: he was drunk, but that was his private affair, in a line with the difference between scrounging and stealing, and now a lifetime spent in keeping everything orderly helped him. He kept himself seated; but at the same time managed to give an impression of standing up by arranging the creases of his trousers, one leg smartly after the other.

The Mrs Toveys were saying:

'So you'll let her take the keys a minute?'

'I said it's not regular,' he growled, staring at her severely from rheumy eyes.

'You look as if you've had a not-regular drop yourself, you old—'

'I expect as you're referring to my sick state, my wound, Mrs Tovey. Wound, madam,' he repeated, glad of this dignified truth.

'Wound my—' she stopped herself. 'Still, you'll look after her, won't you? We've all had a drop too much.'

'Speak for yourself.'

'I've got eyes in my head,' she said.

'No kid? I thought they was fried eggs,' Bletch

allowed himself. His bloodshot eyes glared and he expanded his chest.

'Well they ain't got the cock's tread in 'em like some,' tossed the two Mrs Toveys. 'Now I got to make myself scarce. I'm all behind.'

Bletch lowered his eyes to her hips. 'It's you what says so,' he grunted.

With a sniff and a bang the Mrs Toveys vanished— and were replaced by a vision of Sandras.

'Oh, sergeant,' Sandra said appealing.

Bletch's eyes appraised sternly over their wet red crescents, as over half spectacles. Yet he was chuckling inside, he had scored off Tovey and now this young miss had come, a sight for sore eyes if you like. Yet it paid to look grim.

'Honestly—I won't be a tick with them, sarge.'

He tightened his jaw.

'It's irregular,' he grunted, 'but in your case, Miss—' and he reached round to a cupboard behind him where keys hung inside on secret hooks.

He rose, and corrected a lurch with soldierly care. Then said suddenly:

'But I don't know as Mr Deane's gone. I didn't see 'im go.'

'Oh, he's gone twenty minutes.'

'Funny. The guvnor—he ordinary says goodnight—'

'He was in a hurry.'

Bletch thought: Then I was down the pisshole. But I bet he's still up there. Gone to them other offices he knows. I wouldn't miss him on a night like this, would I?

Not when the half dollars are handing out, not me. But he nevertheless moved towards Sandra, dangling the keys up by his face.

Sandra moved back out of the doorway. Bletch came out smiling like a big old boy, artful.

'And what'll you give me?' he said dangling.

Sandra pretended to giggle: 'Oh, sarge, you *are*,'

Bletch took a quick look either way up and down the passage. He did not see Bone still standing in the shadow of the lift-grill, he saw hardly anything.

He dangled the keys. Sandra saw just keys and face, the rest all round like fog, and her head muzzy and only set on what seemed now of terrible urgency, keys and Tovey and pants—so that when Bletch put his arms round her grunting, 'Come on, now, it's not the first time,' and she saw his cheese-coloured teeth near and his old eyes not smiling but dull as if he was looking at something inside him, she raised her face with a loving sneer, all fallen woman, all sacrifice, and then shut tight her eyes as rum and Bletch came down on her.

Blackness for long gone seconds as Bletch scrabbled and sucked. Then he lost himself and lurched a hand at his trousers.

Her sense snapped alert, she struggled, he began to drag her back into his hole and then lost grip and she grabbed the keys and pushed herself away from him.

They both stood panting, glaring at each other. Agile with fright, she saw suddenly very plainly the calendar-hung battered hole and its old man, red-eyed, now with lipstick on his white stubble—and caught a new look of fear on his face. She felt all right again, she pitied him.

'You better look out, you dirty old pig,' she said low, and ran away to the stairs.

'Sod it,' he breathed to himself, 'you bloody old fool. What about your bleeding waterworks? What about your pension?'

He shouted politely up the stairs, for anyone to hear: 'I trust you find it, miss.'

She ran straight into Bone. He was pressing himself back against the stairs. He had seen it all. He had wanted to rush in and break up Bletch—but she had seemed willing. He stood hating her, Bletch, himself, everything, sickened and emasculated. As she passed he just whispered:

'I saw you.'

She was flustered, she had no time for him.

'Go home to your mummy, darling.' she shouted.

He saw her lips smeared wide with lipstick like tomato soup, and heard again that treasured word 'darling' in such a tone that it finished him. As she clattered on upstairs, he put a fist to his mouth and gave one high clenched sob before running out past Bletch's hole to the door and fresh air.

Bletch looked out anxiously.

'Oh no, oh no,' he said, watching the flying figure and seeing his pension vanish with it.

Up she ran through the echoing stairwell to where Allasol's lights still shone. Holding those obsessive keys tight, revolted by Bletch yet in some compartment proud of herself—her mind still whirled up odd practical thoughts. Funny how young old Bletch had felt, just like anyone else when she shut her eyes; and no man in uniform had ever put his arms round her before—the buttons, the hardness of even that dusty old serge, the peaked cap, they were not so revolting, somehow right. But Bone she had completely forgotten. He had simply passed clean out of mind.

The office had felt dead with only Mrs Tovey there. Now, all alone in it, it came to mysterious life, as if who knows what waited round each corner. She hesitated, listened. An echo in her own ears surged like a sea-shell's. She was breathing hard after the stairs. She thought: The old Red Hell, I'll put myself straight. No—wait till after I've been to H. J.'s room.

She tiptoed quietly over to her own desk. Once there, it was better. Like swimming, getting used to the silence. She took an easy breath, and looked round. The bottles looked thirsty. She poured herself something; it was sweet and sticky, the bottle said Australian Alicante. She made a pursing chirrup with her lips: and Slaughter, now curled up inside a warm new carton put one ear up but kept both eyes firm closed.

'Where've they all gone, Slaughter-puss?' she said gently. She sat on the corner of a desk and lightly hummed: *Yours, Yours, onlee.*

Suddenly Slaughter shot a head like an owl's up from the carton and swung it round at H. J.'s door, ears trumpeted forward; stared a moment, then relaxed, relapsed, licked a paw.

'Silly pussers,' she whispered. 'I must get on with it and go in.'

And all those others were getting on with it—already home or on their way.

Mark Deane sat on leather in his club, dark oils on the walls, the glint of brass and reddish faces around. His fellow-members were all cursing Christmas. Racing interrupted, stock market dulled, relations to see, damned execrable turkey-bird to eat.

Mark nodded, and sipped at his drink. He nodded at the right atmosphere, congratulated himself at having at last got away from that terrible party—and yawned. He got up, and drifted away as Buckland's voice droned along:

'. . . ionic portico, heavily rusticated wings, but a *plain* tympanum . . . I don't know . . .'

And young Sir Gervaise, finely bred son and scion of one of the first families in the country, intoning all over again:

'Can't —ing well see the —ing clock for —ing cards, home's not —ing home any more. . .'

Mark drifted to the window and watched the cabs beetle down St James's. He shrugged his shoulders and slowly shook his head. It was no good. He had to admit it. He would rather be back at Allasol.

Shelagh Nussbaum sat in a coffee bar muttering at her Russian grammar, jigging a foot to the radio's muted beat, and holding the hand of a tousled young man dressed in black suède from neck to foot, who looked away from her half asleep. But she was hungry: and Mom was cooking lokshun soup in the bright new flat in Leman Street, and Dad would be away out on the Guinness.

She snapped the book shut, withdrew her hand:

'Cuttin', man,' she said, and wisely left for the East.

Sue Blair sat alone in a jazz club. Several young men eyed her but never came up, for such a goodlooker was sure to be dated.

Thus Sue spent too much of her time, whenever a loose end came her way, fairest of wall-flowers, lonely and wanted.

Nevile Wrasse had got home on time, turned the lights low and set the long-player with *Yours, Yours* ready. The gin was out, and two glasses. Books and trays blocked every chair, so that only the sofa should be free.

But she was already five minutes late.

Thoroughly prepared and brushed and polished, he did not know what to do in the empty room. He went to the glass, straightened his tie for the third time, and his eyebrows, by nature touching above the bridge of his nose, fused further into a dark frown of anxiety. Surely not? Surely she wouldn't stand *him* up?

Sandra slid the yale key into the lock of H. J.'s private office and stepped inside. She fingered for the light switch—then stopped. There was a noise—a kind of soft-shoe shuffle, the regular creaking of a rocking-chair: and something musical, a broken chord from a muffled harp.

The light from Gorland Brothers flushed its reddish pattern on the wall. It brought the outside world in, and for a moment she thought: The window's open, there's low cloud, faraway sounds come near on such nights. It's an engine far away.

But then her eyes grew used to the dusk and caught a movement round the corner of the desk—a white-shirted back on the old leather sofa, a man's, H. J.'s.

The poor man appeared to be sobbing. He was stretched out at full length as if he had thrown himself down in anguish. He seemed to be burrowing into the sofa to stifle his tears. Or was he in pain? Sandra let out a little O-sound—then stifled it, but too late. Something shot up from underneath H. J. It was Monica. The sofa springs played a loud lyrical burst, and Sandra suddenly found all the nerve in the world and thumped on the light.

Her fingers missed the main switch, all that went on was a pair of frosted glass candles, wan and yellow, high on the farther wall. These cast a dull and dusty light, like the cold end of a summer's evening, on H. J. lumbering slowly over and up, as if awakening from sleep, pulling his clothes together.

Monica in her underclothes switched a hand to right her shoulder strap, put another to pat her hair. Together they sat surprised and tousled, close together, like ship-wrecked figures in a lifeboat.

'Excuse me,' Sandra said, walking forward, 'I'm sure.'

She was smiling very sweetly. She had forgotten her lips were a smear of tomato-soup—she looked like a clown or perhaps a person troubled with lupus.

But it was her moment. She was brilliant. She had command of every muscle in her body, she held herself erect and magnificent, with the sure wide-shouldered walk of a first-class mannequin; certainty and presence in every movement, and inside she burned with delight.

'Oh!' said Monica over and over again, 'Oh! Oh! Oh!' drumming her feet on the floor, as if she wanted to run away from herself.

Then she burst into tears. Her face with its sob-stretched lips looked strangely like Sandra's.

But as suddenly she stopped and cried to H. J.

'*Do* something, Pussy!'

He looked as if a knife had cut him.

'What on earth does this mean, Miss Lee?' he said sternly.

Sandra said pleasantly, looking particularly at nowhere:

'I'm sorry, I *thought* the party was over. I forgot something.'

'Forgot something? This is my private office!'

She gave him a big smile:

'I should know *that*, Mr Deane.'

And she whipped her pants out of the waste-paper basket.

'I forgot my panties,' she said coyly, her heart beating like a big gold drum.

'Oh!' said Monica.

'Really—there are limits, Miss Lee!' H. J. said.

'That's just what I said, Mr Deane. Don't you remember?'

He turned quick to Monica:

'The girl's off her head,' he said wearily.

'Those came off somewhere else,' Monica said and edged away from him.

Sandra gave the pants a little flutter then stuffed them into her bag. She stood armoured in her dress against those two half-clothed. Delight flooded her through and through. The Gorland Brothers sign suffused her with a warm red glow. She had done it!

Monica suddenly screamed:

'My clasp! You were in here! So it *was* you!'

Sandra gave her a long low smile. She could now afford to be in the diamond-racket too.

'Miss Lee, I must ask you to leave,' H. J. said, standing up for better authority and then quickly sitting down as he remembered his disarray. 'I mean leave altogether. The office. Your job. You can call on the cashier after Christmas. That'll be all.'

He looked grim. It had cost him a deal of effort. In any case he always hated sacking people, knowing how much worse the replacement could be.

'It's all right,' Sandra said coolly, 'I was going anyway. Thank you for my time at Allasol. It's been an education if nothing else.' And then she added, 'Pussy'.

'Get out!' screamed Monica, breathing so hard she went up and down like a dummy.

Sandra walked across the room, out of Gorland's light, slim and erect and perfectly poised. She pointed a delicate finger at the light switch:

'Off again?' she said sweetly.

'No!' Monica yelled.

'Tch.'

And she switched off the light and heard Monica scream: 'Switch it on, switch it on, Godfrey, I'll kill you for this, I'll . . . I'll . . . switch it on . . . I'll,' before she quietly closed the door.

As the voice went on and on, higher and higher, like a terrible machine gathering energy, she bent herself double with laughter.

'Oh—oh—' she groaned, 'and was it worth it? Was it *worth* it? Her face!'

She kicked a leg this way, a leg that, in a sudden little step-dance. Slaughter put his ears back and ran away under a desk.

'Poof!' she said to the empty office, to all the stale alcohol and smoke. 'Let's get going! Goodbye Allasol!' she said to her desk in general: and to an old piece of grey ink-eraser that had hung about her tray for as long as she could remember, 'and goodbye *you*!'

She hurried off to the Red Hell, where she quickly slipped her pants on. Tomato-soup lips faced her in the pink glass, and she broke down laughing again. 'Was *her* face red! Is *mine*!'—and then as suddenly stared gravely into the big greyish eyes yearning at her and gave a knowing shake of her head to these lifelong friends. 'Oh, Sandra,' she whispered, admonishing with affection.

But there was no time to waste. She creamed off the tomato, tossed back her hair, and started swiftly on a new face. Greases, powders, colours were tickled and dabbed into place, a smooth painting of herself grew in the glass, lips mouthing strangely, eyes winking and fluttering, and all around the lavatory's quiet echo. Then the hair, this way, that, fingers moving quicker than thoughts.

She straightened her belt and turned sideways to the glass, patting in her stomach and sidling towards it like a bullfighter, then away again, short steps. The sight of the dress suddenly brought back Nevile Wrasse. She laughed again. This paid Nevile out too. Teach him a lesson, too, with his parcel-tricks. That old dress! Why, she'd have hundreds of new dresses now! She was rich, she was secure—she was going to be m-a-r-r-i-e-d!

Out for the last time from the Red Hell, hat and coat and transistor and book, and whoosh along the corridor and down the stone steps again, round and round the empty lift-shaft to the bottom.

Bletch? He'd just better show himself! She whisked clattering past his hole without a glance. But Bletch's voice fearful yet remembering its duty, came after her:

'The key, miss? You got the key?'

She turned at the street door:

'It's in good hands,' she shouted, 'Mr Deane's and Miss Naseby's. How about *that*?'

She slammed the door on a despairing cry as Bletch, feeling his pension finally disappear, at last allowed his military bearing to crumble, took out his teeth, and buried his head in these and his hands.

It was seven o'clock, the streets were quieter, most people had gone home. Only an occasional thrum of stamping and singing still came from yellow-lit pubs with their doors fast shut against the winter night.

Sandra stumped along on her high heels jubilant. The

gothic escarpment of tall insurance buildings and the towering glass of newer office blocks cut against a plum-coloured night-sky: pitted between two immense structures, a small classic church hung back darkly, like a chessman deep in thought. She slipped on a white mistletoe berry, damned it joyfully, and bubbled to think once again: My, what birds with one stone! And such a bitchy, bitchy trick—at last, it seemed, something to remember for ever, ever afterwards. Perhaps sitting jewelled on a white elephant in Sarawak.

To confirm her new joy arose a deep affection for Bun. She saw how tenderly she had always loved him, she hoped they were not hurting him—and, with a gulp of apprehension, that he would still be there. Better to ring his room again? But the thought of talking to those housecoated women put her off. Anyhow—what really could go wrong now?

She caught a bus. She was smiling to herself, so the conductor smiled at her.

'Who's swallowed the canary?' he said. 'Lucky little bird.'

'A Sixpenny,' she laughed, 'that's who.'

It was the wrong bus, it rushed her into the beginning of big shopping streets. She got off, not minding at all. There was both no time and all the time in the world. She zig-zagged along through the last-minute shopping crowd—it was like coming from graven Sunday into a blazing week-night—hugging transistor and book to her tummy and holding her head back free and wild.

A woman, pushed by two happy men carrying straw-bags from which birds' heads lolled, dropped her parcels and her bag. Sandra knelt down to help her. The woman's bag had opened and a lipstick rolled out.

'Why, it's one of ours!' Sandra cried among all the feet. 'It's Ruby Nearness!'

The woman looked sharply into her eyes.

'Yours?' she said tartly. 'A helping hand's all very well but there's limits. That's *mine*.'

'*There* we are!' Sandra said, giving her the last parcel.

She stood up, and a man who had been dodging to pass glared at her.

'Have you got *all* day, miss?' he said.

She looked him in eyes, and, slowly and with wonder, said:

'Why, yes. Yes, I *have*.'

The man's jaw dropped open. Sandra saw traffic-lights green and hurried across the road to get another bus. There was a small queue—and instantly she found she had not got all day, not at all, hardly a minute.

She stamped an impatient foot at the queue, felt softness, looked down, and there was a piece of coloured rubber balloon again. All day she seemed to have been seeing the nipples of these broken balloons, bits of mistletoe and holly and berries littering the street. She suddenly felt thirsty—all that afternoon drinking, all this queue. A big pub bellied its frosted windows just by the stop. Saloon Lounge, it said, and she thought: 'Why not for once?' and went in.

It was not full. This was the day when the workers' pubs were packed, but the shoppers' pubs at ease. She ordered a gin and tonic, changed her mind and made it just the tonic. She was smiling to herself, shining inside and glowing with it.

A man along the bar smiled, then looked down not to appear too familiar.

She sipped her drink, and grew impatient of this too. Long twists of coloured tinfoil revolved slowly in light, invisible draughts.

'It's safer to keep off it,' the man said pleasantly, and took a quick drink of his beer.

She answered with ease, as if she knew him.

'Oh, I've had plenty this afternoon. Got to keep my head now, though.'

Sandra finished her drink. She thought the man had nice eyes, yet scarcely took him in. The clock ticked above the small murmur of the few people there. Orange and pink and green garlands hung about the ceiling and mahogany-work, making permanent paper flowers look deader and dustier. The man smiled at her.

'Why don't you have another one—just one more,' he said. 'On me.'

In those few moments he had fallen in love with her, as far as this is possible.

'No, thank you very much,' she said.

'Please,' he said.

She had that particular appearance which fitted his private dream. Once or twice her kind of face had turned up in his life, passed on. But this girl had spoken so easily with him, it was a fatal encounter. He was after no pick-up, he was sincere. He was twenty-eight years old. He was a reasonably good, kind fellow, with a spark in him but not too much.

'I've got to go off to the Bughouse to see my fiancé,' she said, and left.

She never saw him again. He carried a photograph in his mind for months afterwards of this beautiful girl so tragically bound to a madman. Occasionally it came to mind, in the years that followed, clear and saddening but treasured.

Had this occurred an hour earlier, what might not have happened? Now, she took a taxi.

Homeward bound too were others—a sad Bone suffering the poignant torture of youth, a hole in his heart, hopeless, had looked in at his bike as he passed round to the back door for kipper-smelling tea.

Glinting black and silver she stood like a racer quiet in the low creosoted shed. Away in the dark sky a church-tower pealed lonely practice-bells. Bone took the flashlamp and passed its strong beam over his machine, bringing glints of chromium and a gleaming of darker metal strength, of fresh leather and blacktread tyres; underneath lay her droppings of oil on the concrete. Oilfat youth passed its beam lovingly over this oily other love: and as he did so, he ceased to suffer so much. Alone with his machine, which he could trust, he became more a man than he knew, as mature as many a grown man in love first with his car, and only secondly his wife.

Bossom was already home, rubber-cemented to his

favourite comedian on the telly. His mother and father were out, gliding with prize-winning cross-steps through hesitation waltzes at the Palais.

As Bossom stared into the little blue screen, his face imitated every contortion of Ted Trafalgar's, and his lips repeated adeptly each well-timed wise-cracking line. He was studying. In time to come he would probably do well. Indeed, at the moment he was rather funnier than Trafalgar himself. Slapped across his bruised eye there quivered a brown and bloody raw-cut sliver cut from one of the legs of the family turkey.

Wrasse had given Sandra up. He put the gin away for a future occasion.

What to do now? He went over and looked at himself again in the mirror. Not so bad. But the room accused him with its emptiness. It had always been empty in feeling, every piece of furniture having been seconded to him by his mother, nothing of his own choice. It was an allowance-man's room. He needed all his cash to keep himself around the clubs and restaurants: he never bought anything. Decoration was supplied by old samples of the accessories he sold, morocco-bound books that contained cigarettes, a silver frigate that burst into flame to light the affluent cigarette, an ashtray made of golfballs, and many a Toby Jug.

He stood reviewing the little drinking clubs on his list. But he could not choose. He was upset. One plan gone wrong suggested that everything else would fail. He wandered over to 'his books'—somebody's Concise

Encyclopaedia—and took down the volume S-Z. This contained paragraphs on sex and venereal disease. Over and over again he had read these simple items, feasting on them in a compulsive way, habitually expectant and always frustrated. Yet he fingered the leaves with another love, for he did feel them as books, his *books*, real ones not filled with cigarettes; sometimes he sensed a grave feeling of aesthetic pleasure. Moreover, his chosen items often lead his eye to read others. He knew a lot about Venezuela.

Later, he thought he would go out and take in a couple of Tastyburgers before seeing what the night and Earl's Court had to offer.

The night for Olle and Jill was already in full swing. They had begun at a cocktail-dansant. Jill was worried about her clothes, but kept her mind on her pearls and thanked her lucky stars that there were bars and butteries as well as restaurants. Olle was shovelling out pound notes—yet picking up each bill and carefully storing it away—and glad of it, glad to be out with a presentable girl in a city bigger than his own. What came of it did not matter so much.

Jill was in 'seventh heaven'. This wonderful smasher offered a romantic foreign-ness which fitted an ideal she had never realised before. She flowered, yet her pre-servative instincts yelled: Keep, keep this moment—so that when for instance she felt 'woozy' she decidedly drank tomato juice and thus the evening would be kept at its athletic best and go on for ever and ever, what joy.

While Olle would be willingly fleeced by waiters, taxis, barmen well into the night. Besides, this was an *interesting* as well as a pretty girl. Wide interests. No elephants, he was assured, in Sarawak. None at all.

When Sandra paid off her taxi she was still smiling to herself, still shining so that yet another passing man looked back at her with quickened interest, infected by her look of happiness. This lovely lack of self-consciousness brought the immediate attention she longed for but always repelled with her consciously excitant tricks. Now, being unselfconscious, she never even noticed the man.

At the clinic, a man in a dark coat and white collar—a doctor? a porter?—said he knew very well about the exceptional Mr Stanbetter. A most exceptional man to be here at such an exceptional hour on such an exceptional night—not that he was taking exception . . . but this man too in his official jacket was powerless to refuse her and asked her to step into an ante-room.

This was furnished in smooth and shining modern taste, she sat down with pleasure on a little lemon-yellow paper-clip of a chair. A pile of tattered magazines sat on the shining clean table like a quiet nest of germs. On the wall hung a chart with drawings of several small beasts not unlike the Warble Fly and labelled haematozoon: an unplaced memory rose up, she whisked it away. Bun, she thought, Bun—I'm going to snuggle up to him, and *teach* him, and see he grows up, the big baba.

And then there he was at the door, pale with toxics.

To fix him with proud eyes? To announce in telling tones her momentous decision? Or to hang her head and shyly but yet with mischief murmur, in a 'little' voice, her submission?

'O Bun!' she yelled, running to him, 'O Bun dear, I will!'

'Ouch,' Bun said, freeing his ill arm.

'Bun, I'm coming with you to Sarawak! We'll be married, Bun! Here and now!'

Bun looked round the room, at the haematozoon, at the carefully bright colours.

'Here?' he said.

He had had a hard day, with all his plans put out, with frustration and anger and then long pains of forgiveness and understanding—all of which he had had to face alone—and with new decisions, and with these injections. Now a great cleansing sense of patience filled him, of manliness and endurance endured. His eyes clouded with relief as he smiled down at her as she talked on:

'I've left Allasol—I'll tell you later. I'm free. When can we go? How's your poor self, did they hurt you?'

She frowned as if she would go straight up and give those doctors a piece of her mind. Both in this, and in the way she had announced her decision, there was the sure note of possessiveness: together with his pleased patience, they might have already been married for years.

'It's nothing much,' he said. 'I say, now you'll have to be done too!' He smiled down at her: 'Oh, Sandra, I'm so glad,' he said. And sniffed: 'I say, you do smell lovely!'

'Smell? Oh—It's Moujik,' she said. 'Bun, we're going out! We're going to have a wonderful dinner and celebrate!'

'I've got to lie down,' Bun said.

She whispered into his tie:

'Then let's lie down.'

And raised her large and beautiful soft greyish eyes with such meaning that their message welled out beyond the bars of mascara, the walls of coloured grease.

'Yes,' he said, as she raised her lips, 'yes.'

H. J. and Monica had each gone their separate ways, she to Brighton hard with anger and with hopelessness. It had been hopeless all along: now this ordinary bestial exhibition had shown the whole thing up. She felt cheap. And the emptiness which she would have wished to be forlorn and tender instead weighed like a stone that grew only harder and harder. She was alone with it. No one could know. Only, in a way the stone helped her: she decided to go straight to the theatre, if only for two acts.

H. J. started out on the drive home to his wife and topiary in Surrey with some relief, for he was simply tired out. Would it all be forgotten, he wondered, like other parties which seem afterwards more like some dreamy film remotely viewed than part of real life lived in the flesh? Mavis, Ralph, Hearst, Sandra—now Monica: staff, staff, staff. And at the back of his mind there buzzed, too, that ever-present Fly.

He suddenly felt too done in to drive. He turned the

car about and drove it back to a central garage. Tired, tired out—and so he went to a strip club.

Crust Skivers, he thought, looking at a pale pink haunch a yard from his eye, Pickled Fleshers. But sitting there, a strange sensation came over him. He felt that queer disembodied certainty we feel sometimes about places visited for the first time—the 'I have been here before feeling'.

Well, he knew he had. But it was not quite like that. This was a creepy feeling. Sitting there among all the flesh, he felt queer pains of the spirit. He tried to concentrate. But he was quite upset. Where had he seen, quite recently, a naked girl? He would definitely see his doctor after Christmas.

Mrs Tovey feeling tipsy had abandoned her round of gentlemen for her man at home. Together now, hand in hand, he in his chair and she on a tubular steel tele-stool, they sat in the blue tele-twilight watching Ted Trafalgar, an old green aspidistra in its china window-pot haunting the lace curtains behind.

On the other side of London Mavis Cook sighed with pleasure in her quiet and neat room. Her head ached from the afternoon wine, it buzzed with memories she would rather forget, and she put them aside, as for long she had learned to. Now she dabbed the last traces of junket from her lips, and surveyed securely and with more fondness than most people all the holly-green parcels arranged on the bed, each tied with ribbonned label and gold-red string, each less a simple Christmas gift than a real attachment to relations and friends near and far, for they were needed and valued.

'Hello all!' Quentin piped to any of his family who might be within earshot of the hall, and passed through to his boiler to rake out loveable clinker, to listen to her draw freshly, to feed her with grains.

Affected by the spirit of Christmas, Tiny Hearst decided to give himself a holiday from wearing out his old dinner-jacket for supper.

He put on his slipper-socks, lit his gas fire, reached across to the refrigerator and took out ham and cheese and bread and onions, settled these on a tray by his armchair, and added from his pocket a big bag of bulls-eyes. He glanced for a moment at his dead wife's photograph in the silver frame, and thought comfortably what each evening in a friendly way he thought: Presence is better than company.

Then he reached up behind the big brown regimental group photograph on the mantelpiece for what was hidden there, *The Sunbathing Gazette*. It was very quiet. The gas fire hissed steadily. Traffic rumbled, regular. He filled his mouth with ham and cheese and onions, eased his trousers, and opened the pages.

Abruptly the room was filled with voices. He shot up in the chair, plunging the magazine beneath him.

'Peace on earth,' sang youths in the porch outside his window, 'and goodwill to all men.'

Hearst listened hard at the house passage outside his own flat. Presently, footsteps sounded, someone was opening the front door. The singing stopped. Chink of money. Talk, goodnights. Hearst nodded, sighed out a breath of relief, and returned to his studies.

In the Tropical Medicine Clinic, under the haematozoon chart, Bun and Sandra kissed, eyes closed.

It was she, a few moments later, who whisked out a handkerchief and wiped lipstick from his lips.

And it was she who said:

'Let's go.'

To where that night she was to 'become a woman', though this, in every crucial way, she had surely become in the last and full flowering of the ended hour.